PORTS OF HELL

JOHNNY STRIKE

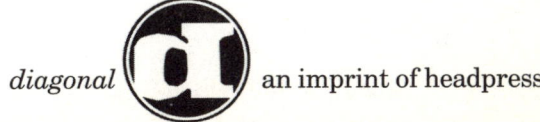

diagonal an imprint of headpress

A DIAGONAL BOOK
Published in 2004
by Headpress

Headpress / Diagonal
PO Box 26
Manchester
M26 1PQ
Great Britain

(tel) +44 (0)161 796 1935
(fax) +44 (0)161 796 9703
(e) info.headpress@zen.co.uk
(w) www.headpress.com

PORTS OF HELL
Text copyright © Johnny Strike
This volume copyright © 2004 Headpress
Artwork and cover illustration © Claudio Parentela
Layout & design: Walt Meaties & David Kerekes

World Rights Reserved

All rights reserved. No part of this book may be reproduced or utilised in any form, by any means, including electronic, mechanical and photocopying, or in any information storage or retrieval system, without prior permission in writing from the publishers.

British Library Cataloguing in Publication Data
A catalogue record for this book is available from the British Library

ISBN 1-900486-33-4

PORTS OF HELL

JOHNNY STRIKE

Special thanks to Oliveira Mattos for his editing of even the first stack of raw notes.

Thanks to Michael Lucas and Bruce Barnard for their help in fine tuning the manuscript as it neared completion.

Thanks to David Kerekes for publishing the book.

For Jane

Part One

CALIFORNIA

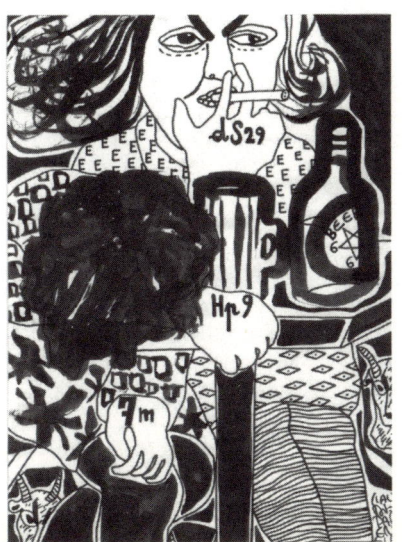

Jamie crossed a leg and looked at Elias, who was sitting across from him wearing makeup and a lavender turban. Elias was heavyset, wore a pencil thin moustache, had a shaved head and claimed he was from Lemuria. He had the most compelling pale blue eyes Jamie had ever seen.

As though laying out a card hand Elias placed money, credit cards, an airline ticket and a passport on a table between them. It was Jamie's picture on the passport but a different name. Elias wanted Jamie to become an agent and go to Thailand on a training mission.

PORTS OF HELL

When Jamie first arrived in San Francisco he had taken a room in a seedy hotel in the Tenderloin. He spent each morning watching the hordes of homeless move by on the street below. On this particular day he opened the blinds to see a phalanx of shopping carts. They were packed with all their owners' Earthly belongings. They were being led by a man who pushed an oxygen tank. A few in wheelchairs were being rolled along like some aberrant royalty of the gutter. Others hobbled on canes with dirty bedrolls slung over shoulders. They talked to themselves and looked for butts on the ground. One old crone who used a filthy crutch stopped, looked up and made a gesture as if beckoning Jamie to join them.

Jamie stood at the window thinking about the last twenty folded up and tucked away in his wallet behind his driver's license. A week before he had fallen in with a couple of three card monte players. They'd taught him to be a shill, which included winning and losing strategically as well as being able to talk to and prompt the players. They worked the street fairs and shows where they'd pay their way in and set up in the men's room. They were chased by the police a few times but never caught. When the other two started to talk about a robbery he had parted company.

A few blocks from his hotel Jamie entered the waiting room of an old doctor's office. Two other customers were there: an elderly woman who looked at a wall and muttered and an equally elderly man with darting eyes who snapped his mouth open and shut like a wooden dummy. Jamie stepped out to the lobby for a smoke. When he returned the waiting room was empty.

A voice called out "Next," and he curiously entered the private office that resembled a pawn shop. TVs and VCRs were displayed on shelves. Greasy boxes overflowing with cameras and tape recorders were stacked against a wall. A lone motorized wheelchair sat parked in another corner. The doctor wore dark glasses and sat behind his desk and fiddled with a gold watch. He asked Jamie what he wanted. Jamie mumbled about some vague back pain and how Codeine # 4's had always helped. The doctor named a price and wrote out a prescription. He snatched the ten dollar bill with crooked fingers stained by tobacco and pointed to another door. Jamie could sell these easily to Bones, the junkie handyman at the hotel.

Jamie walked a few blocks to a bus stop and took one to the Mission district. He walked down a reeking sidewalk. He

Part One

stepped past a pile of black feces, a pool of purple vomit, the remains of a discarded sugar drink in a plastic pouch and a bus stop that was a pile of green shattered glass. He passed a series of low roofed restaurants with outside seating. At one table three furtive men guarding their drinks glanced his way. The neighborhood was full of bars, taquerias and dirty looking cafes. All afternoon and part of the evening Jamie searched for a job but without luck. Then, below a red neon DINER sign a waitress, cigarette dangling from her mouth, was taping up a Help Wanted sign in the window.

Jamie looked in. There were nine tables in a blue room trimmed in gaudy yellow with a counter along a wall. A pimply faced boy was perched on a stool with a cup of coffee. A fat man slouched at a table, the remains of a spaghetti dinner sat before him. Jamie went in. The waitress who had retreated to a back alcove, reappeared, smiled weakly and pointed to an empty table. Jamie asked about the job and with an air of disdain she told him to go to the back and look for Sammy.

Into a steam-filled hell he stepped where pots and pans bobbed in sinks of greasy, soapy water. A rack of dishes rolled out of an industrial machine with a blast of steam and an apparition emerged: a wiry man with dagger eyes, beak nose, wearing a tight white T-shirt and white pants. At first Jamie was startled. Sammy's head resembled some ugly, prehistoric bird. The bird man pushed a button and the machine droned to a stop.

"Who sent you back here?"

He ignored Jamie's silence and gave him a quick assessment.

"Alright," he said, "I'll introduce ya to the beast."

He showed Jamie the operation but had the annoying habit of adding "see what I mean?" after nearly every sentence: "The dishes come in here, see what I mean? Now you clean 'em off, and line 'em up like this, see what I mean? Now check this switch. Push this button. See what I mean?"

Finding this annoying yet strangely compelling, Jamie paid scant attention to what Sammy was saying and instead listened for the see-what-I-means. This would cause him difficulties the first day on the job. The bird man said the last guy had worked both the day and night shifts and asked if Jamie would do the same until he could find a second dishwasher. Jamie hesitated for only a moment. He was nearly broke.

After a few days Sammy hired a man who looked to be somewhere between sixty-five and seventy-five. The new old guy took days while Jamie worked the busier night shift.

It was dull work, the food was lousy and Jamie couldn't figure out why the place was popular. At times he didn't think there'd be an end to the hard rubber pans of dirty dishes dumped in front of him. Or an end to the rank, nameless smell that permeated the back rooms. Or an end to Sammy's foul temper. The cook, a pleasant Nicaraguan, hated Sammy so much he finally quit. Sammy took over behind the grill.

As the weeks passed Jamie started to save some money. He had little expenses and took his meals at work. But one night he showed up slightly drunk after a visit with an off-again on-again girlfriend. He took a blurred look around at all the pans of dirty dishes. He decided he had had it. He walked out the back door.

Lou, the desk clerk at Jamie's hotel was an irritable old man with a foul mouth. He squinted at the Racing Forum. "Goddamn it I'll give you your fuckin' receipt," he barked, "Just wait a goddamn minute." Jamie could smell the alcohol on his breath and resisted the impulse to give a him a jab. Tomorrow he would take a bus out to Yellow Cab. He had seen a "drivers wanted," ad in the evening paper.

The Yellow Cab building was massive, with no front entrance. He walked to the back and found a lot dotted with banana yellow taxicabs. There were gas pumps to one side and a car wash on the other. There was a half enclosed area with some benches, a dispatcher's booth, lockers and a bathroom. He felt he was about to enlist in some strange army.

At the main office he was buzzed through. Behind a desk, at a computer, sat a man with bushy hair and a beard. He grunted, handed him an application and with a thick Russian accent instructed Jamie to get a DMV printout, sign up at the Hall of Justice for a class on driving laws, another class at Yellow, then pay the insurance. Jamie would be given a badge and a set of keys after he had done all that. Back on the lot, Jamie watched a cab roll in. The driver looked exhausted.

A week later in the early morning Jamie waited at a bus stop. An old character in a plaid suit stumbled out of a rundown hotel weaving a path towards a couple of imposing prostitutes working the next corner. At a restaurant a ghost of a waiter delivered a cup of coffee and eggs over rice. Frowning, he flipped on a dim overhead lamp and looked out the window at two winos in a phone booth sharing a bottle. In the

Part One

entrance of an old apartment building a pimp in a gold satin suit lit his cigar. In another doorway a muscular transvestite in a red wig paced back and forth. Jamie boarded the bus, off to his new job.

The yard. Jamie joined the line that formed in front of the dispatcher's window. Drivers talking about gas and gates, meter and a halfs, playing certain neighborhoods and hotels. The dispatcher opened the monkey cage, started to punch cards and toss down medallions, waybills and scoop up all the tips—a steady flow of dollars and fives. The dispatcher didn't seem pleased with the tips. In fact, he didn't seem pleased with anything. Jamie gave him a five. He wanted a new cab and not some unreliable "spare". Out in the lot, in the early morning fog, he searched for his cab with a flashlight. Here and there headlights came on, transforming the place into a kind of urban netherworld.

Jamie drove straight to the airport and pulled into the outdoor bullpen and put the cab in a line. An older driver crabbed his way over and said hello. His cab and hair were shiny and perfect at all times. His nickname was the Groomer. He was in his late sixties, but kept in shape. His hair was dyed jet black.

"Jesus, just listen," he said.

"They speak every goddamn language here but English."

He nodded towards a Filipino driver who, with delicate hands, tossed up pieces of bread high in the air for the circling sea gulls to snatch.

"Look at this fuck feedin' those birds. I'd like to have my shotgun. Those birds shit on my cab and this asshole feeds 'em." He spat into the dust. "They're dirty birds, dirtier than pigeons. Did ya know that?" He was getting worked up.

Even above the traffic noises Jamie could hear the wild screech of the big birds. Jamie enjoined him to listen too.

"You're outta your fuckin' mind," he said giving Jamie a disgusted look. He headed back to his cab and began to polish it.

Jamie pulled up to International, found a fare and loaded a pile of awkwardly taped up packages into the trunk. The owners of the packages were two Germans in gray flannel suits. They muttered to each other as Jamie delivered them to the Federal building.

Morning at the yard. Under the harsh yellow light Frank, a moody ex-con, took one step at a time trying not to spill a styrofoam cup of scalding coffee. The previous night two drivers had fought over a fare at Pier 23. They had pulled guns and shot

PORTS OF HELL

at each other from their cabs. One driver was dead from a head wound, the other was in jail. Frank knew the guy in jail. Jamie and Frank decided to play the same hotel and headed out in a drizzle.

Jamie found that weapons were common with drivers: handguns, stun guns, knives, screwdrivers, mace, clubs and crazy weapons like sword canes and sword umbrellas. Frank showed him how to use a clipboard by shoving it into the attacker's throat and cutting off the windpipe. Another driver told him a dubious story of how he had used the cab itself, or rather his driving ability, to throw a robber from the cab.

But Jamie knew that most of the time you didn't have a chance to use your weapon: your potential attacker was behind you or next to you. He was told that the best defense was being savvy enough to simply not pick them up. Frank said that he would develop a nose for this but he could still be fooled. There was a couple with a baby who worked out of top flight hotels. Another guy worked the airport, bus and train stations and carried a dummy suitcase. Another nut randomly shot drivers in the head. Another used the seat belt to strangle them. Jamie found the job exhausting. He drove a hundred or so miles per shift: stopping, starting, in and out of the cab, loading luggage, unloading, traffic jams, bad drivers, irate drivers, near accidents, accidents, angry faces in rear view mirrors.

Radio call. Bar in the Sunset District. Through the door came a dark figure dressed in a ratty brown leather jacket and matching hat. He brought with him the musty smell of unwashed clothes, cigarettes: something poisonous lingered in there too. Strong chiseled face, eyes hidden under his hat. In a syrupy voice he named an address across town, settled back, lit a cigarette and asked if Jamie knew anything about snakes. He proceeded to tell Jamie about the Texas rattlesnake roundups of his youth. "Now they'd shoot gasoline through copper tubing with a garden weeder into a rocky area they figured some rattlers were holed up. Sometimes hundreds would come out. Then they'd toss 'em into a tote sack. At the jamboree there'd be handlers in high leather boots and they'd put on little shows like pop balloons with their fangs, then milk 'em, cut off their heads, hang 'em, gut 'em, and strip 'em for boots, belts, and hat bands. And the meat they'd can and put some kind of a gourmet label on it."

Jamie took another radio call. At the entrance of a small hotel

Part One

a gray, wisp of a man wearing horn rimmed glasses perched low on his nose stepped out from behind some bushes and gave a little wave.

"I'm Doctor Hunter," he said, "I called. I need to get up to the Russian River. Do you know it?"

Excited, Jamie lied and said yes. It was a two hundred dollar fare. He got out the map, located the area and the most direct route. The doctor was quiet during the drive so he found what sounded like incidental theater music on the radio and settled into the freeway drive.

"Would you like to hear a story, strange but true?"

Jamie turned the radio off.

"A few years back I was part of an ecological tour, in the jungles of Guatemala. We, that is the expedition, came across something quite spectacular."

The time had somehow flown by and Jamie made note of the upcoming turnoff.

"Hm-m... well, what was it?"

"One of the Visitors. And very much alive."

Jamie laughed but a shiver of recognition shot through him and he felt just a moment of panic. He looked in the rearview mirror at Hunter who was staring out the window.

"The Visitor stepped from a crashed capsule and floated away," Hunter said. "Our government showed up with a faceless team called the Committee. We were interviewed by their so called specialists. Then they sent us back to our appointed universities."

"I must find them!" Hunter became overexcited.

"Er... where?"

"They're here. They're definitely here."

Who was this character? Jamie looked at him again in the rear view mirror; his trimmed mustache twitched back and forth.

When Jamie asked what the Visitor had looked like Hunter fell off into mumbling to himself.

Jamie pulled over at a smart cottage surrounded by red rose bushes in full bloom. With an inquisitive smile Hunter studied him. He paid handsomely, stepped lively from the cab and disappeared behind the door of the cottage.

As Jamie crossed a bridge the sun sent a shaft of light through the tree tops. Tents were scattered along the shoreline and in the river stood fishermen in knee-high boots and hats. A part of him wondered what their lives were like. He imagined them later, around the campfire, eating the delicious fish. He thought about Dr. Hunter.

At a stylish hotel a limousine cruised up and parked in front of him. The driver got out and had a smoke with a bellhop. Together they aimed mechanical smiles towards the main entrance where a doorman opened one of the swinging glass doors for a fashionable lady. She descended the steps and headed towards Jamie's cab. In response to the snub, the limousine driver whipped out a cell phone and made a call. The bellhop bowed awkwardly, walked ahead of her and opened the back door. She eased in, took off her dark glasses and hat.

She wanted a tour of the city. Jamie explained the hourly rate but she stopped him, opened her purse and handed him three crisp hundred dollar bills. He drove her through Golden Gate Park; in the Haight Ashbury she lit a clove cigarette. Jamie showed her the Golden Gate Bridge, the "crookedest" street and Alcatraz. At Coit Tower he waited while she went to the top. Throughout the tour she had remained silent. Finally she instructed him to return to the hotel. Jamie watched her disappear behind the swinging glass doors.

At South Beach he pulled into a parking lot to have his lunch. He turned off the engine and was at ease in the solitude. He looked out across the water to Oakland.

A dark sedan pulled in and a bald man in a tuxedo stepped out of the back and headed towards him. He was heavy-set but comfortable with the weight, the way some men are. There was something familiar about him but Jamie couldn't put his finger on it. Had he been a fare? He had a large face, thin lips, full nose and smooth youthful skin. His pencil thin mustache and false eyelashes added a theatrical touch and softened the intensity of his pale blue eyes. There was something vaguely simian about him. He smiled, showed small white teeth and handed Jamie a card.

He walked back to the sedan. The door was still opened, awaiting him. The card was embossed with the name Elias and an address at the elegant Hotel Red Star. On the other side 7 P.M. was printed neatly. How unlikely. But there had been something undeniably intriguing about the man. What did he want? Jamie would be there to find out. He decided to leave a note in his message box that said where and whom he had gone to see.

When Jamie arrived back at his hotel he found an intoxicated Lou flirting with a streetworn whore who reeked of a repelling floral perfume. Lou made a little dance like movement and mumbled something. The whore smiled, displayed missing teeth, then covered her mouth with her hand.

That evening he went to see this man Elias. A doorman in a

Part One

gold uniform smiled quickly and opened the door with a sweeping gesture. At the front desk a clerk whispered into a phone, squinted suspiciously and hung up. He addressed Jamie in a high pitched voice. Jamie stuck the card under his nose and the clerk's face formed a servile smile barely covering his dormant viciousness. Jamie took an elevator and, at the end of a long, carpeted hallway, found the room number. The door was answered by a man with an oddly slanted mouth wearing a baggy black suit. He had a long face, flat black eyes and slicked back white hair. Elias' driver. He stepped out into the hallway and shut the door behind him.

"I'm Winks," he said extending a bony hand. "Can't see him right now but that gives us time for a drink."

They took the elevator up a few more floors and found a table in the bar. Why the stall? Was this a setup of some sort? Jamie's apprehension mounted when Winks made almost no conversation, but then Jamie got the notion that he was just slightly mad.

The dimly lit room was crowded with plastic plants, to create a jungle atmosphere. Water gurgled in an Oriental fountain near the table. A chirping sound drifted through the room. On a small stage shadows moved back and forth, then disappeared.

An attractive redhead sat at the bar and displayed her shapely legs. There was a thin, pale man at the bar wearing a tropical print shirt. To amuse himself Jamie studied the shirt; yellow palm trees, white coconuts, black ukuleles, gold thatch roofed island huts and red sailboats all floating topsy turvy on electric blue waves. While Winks flagged the waitress for the drinks the shirt moved down the bar closer to the redhead and said something to her. They talked for a few minutes, then got up and left together. Winks turned back the cuff of a heavily starched shirt and looked at a dazzling gold watch with diamonds that circled the face.

They found Elias dressed in a hooded black robe, sitting in an ornate high back chair that might have once belonged to a bishop but for the demonic head carved on top of the tall back. His hand cradled his chin. A soaring sensation rushed through Jamie. He had to steady himself as if too drunk or high. Winks directed him to a seat and he felt a semblance of equilibrium return.

Elias unzipped himself out of the robe. Underneath he wore a dark blue suit, white shirt and red bow tie. He smiled, showing tiny sparkling teeth. He lit

PORTS OF HELL

Jamie's cigarette with a lighter that he seemed to snatch out of the air; it disappeared just as magically. The room was lit in tangerine and brought to Jamie's mind a film set. Winks, over at the bar, mixed more drinks. Jamie continued to feel a pleasant backwards floating sensation. He squinted at Elias, whose face was eerie in the flickering light of an errant lamp. Elias lit a cigar, working it around in his mouth. He seemed to be growing thinner as the shadows moved across the room playing tricks on Jamie.

Elias made a circle with his cigar and set it in the ashtray. He put his fingers together and the shadow it projected resembled a bird. Across the room wearing a long pale face, Winks sat quietly plucking at his sleeve. Elias examined his nails, saw something he didn't like, picked at it, reexamined it and passed inspection.

He drew another circle in the air.

Jamie found himself under a sky thick with stars.

"No need for words," Elias said.

Elias' expression remained unchanged. He drew another circle in the air. The intensity softened with his smile. His expression again turned serious. Jamie's head felt warm, then cool, then warm again.

In just a moment Jamie suddenly knew something. But there were no words for that something. He felt far from civilization and a distant part of him slowly being reborn. Elias said he was from Lemuria and wanted Jamie to join his team. Jamie's first inclination was to laugh but a wave of recognition passed through him and as crazy as Elias' statement was, Jamie knew it was true.

Winks led the way out. The elevator silently delivered them to the garage. The white-capped, white-gloved, attendant caught sight of them, turned and whistled. A moment later the black sedan pulled up and Winks climbed in behind the wheel. Elias had told Jamie he wanted to hire him for a driving job. He wanted Jamie to chauffeur a young lady named Anna to and from her therapy appointments. He had agreed to start the following Saturday.

A few days later a dinner invitation from Elias arrived. It was on an old postcard; a sepia photograph of an American Indian wearing war paint.

The restaurant was in the back of an old hotel in the theater district. With a ghostly air the maitre d' directed Jamie to a private room. He recognized only Elias at the massive table of ten.

Part One

He sat next to an intriguing girl in a V-front black velvet dress. She had striking blue gray eyes and a mouth that looked to be always suppressing a smile. Elias nodded and introduced Anna: the lady who was to attend the therapy appointments. The rest of the faces were a blur of sameness and Elias pulled back into a deep meditation. Anna had little cups of ears which another girl would have tried to hide, but she purposely exposed them, tying back her hair. Jamie liked that. Anna gradually became a bit intoxicated and once put a finger to Jamie's lips. She smiled and pressed her leg against his and took another swallow of wine.

The dinner ended and everyone dispersed. Anna said goodnight and got into a taxi that was in front of the hotel. Jamie walked along the street. She had given him a little nibble on the cheek. Desire set in while he thought about her. The awkwardness of the last girlfriend passed through his thoughts. With Anna, though, he felt that would not happen. They already seemed to have a familiar, warm connection. He knew he was being optimistic but he went ahead and felt that way.

Anna's apartment building had tall, watery green glass doors, pillars covered with scroll work on each side and, directly above the door, a crested balcony with florid leafing. Jamie parked by the entrance early and checked his watch. He lit a cigarette, cracked the window and half listened to the radio dispatcher rattle off the fares. Then, she was coming towards the cab. She had changed her look so much he barely recognized her. She wore a smart Russian fur hat, a short coat and lace up black boots. She gave him an address and got in the back. Jamie played along with the formal mood. At a high rise office building where each floor was an identical row of oblique square windows she got out.

A half hour later she was back. "Jamie, let's go," she said and climbed into the front and fell back into the seat. "To a bar."

Snugly arranged in a private booth she tucked a strand of hair behind an ear. After some cozy looks and small talk, a strange finality appeared in her eyes. She downed a few cocktails but, as the driver, Jamie abstained and instead drank coffee and smoked. She smoked too, one after another.

They continued to go out for drinks after her therapy sessions and other times she would just call to talk. She would go on in a disconnected way about dreams and pet theories and a lot of what she said reminded Jamie of his

PORTS OF HELL

own disjointed journals. She would not discuss Elias except in vague and cryptic ways. Jamie wanted to make love to her but she would only let him kiss her.

At the bar of a quiet tavern where ceiling fans whirled above, Elias, like a contented and noble ape, gently swished his Martini. He showed his small white teeth and took a healthy gulp. His gaze moved down the bar. "Anna stabbed her therapist," he said to Jamie and made a little motion like he was chasing off a fly. Jamie looked concerned. Elias placed a hand on his shoulder.

"I was able to settle the incident without any problems. She'll be away for a while." Elias paid the bill and they began a slow walk through the city. The architecture they passed seemed jagged and cartoonish to Jamie. Within it he knew was a puzzle of corridors, elevators, escalators, tunnels, lobbies and interlocking buildings that mirrored perhaps the pathways that he felt Elias might open in his mind.

In the morning at the Civic Center BART station, Jamie took a train out to the Mission District. He walked to the diner where he had washed dishes. His history there seemed as though from a previous lifetime. He peered in to see Sammy, the bird man, taking an order. Jamie headed in the direction of two Mexican restaurants he liked but found both to have lines of shivering people out to the street. He walked by a long row of sidewalk vendors. In a bar, vibe cocktail music was coming from an invisible sound system. The seats were covered with black velour. The ghoulish bartender who wore goggle-like glasses was shaking up a drink. A few blocks away he stopped at a place he had wondered about. The food on people's plates looked okay so he placed an order. When it arrived it looked as if it was from an entirely different restaurant. The gravy-like soup was tasteless and the pasta and meatball surrounded in a tomato sauce was tasteless too. He left with an unsatisfied feeling, soon forgotten, his attention turning to the cold.

At his hotel Jamie found that Lou was not at his desk. He sensed that something was wrong. A group of old men gloomily shuffled back and forth in the lobby. Jamie asked where Lou was and one of them stepped over, grasped his arm and told him what he already knew: Lou was dead. Heart attack. One of the men, an oldster with pinkish skin and sunglasses that made him resemble a mutated bug creature, pulled out a blurry photograph. It was of himself, Lou and a smiling stripper at some bar. He made sure everyone looked at

Part One

the photo again. Jamie climbed the six flights to his room.

The morning was sunny and the temperature had risen ten degrees. At the front desk a Chinese man with a skeletal grin was looking over some papers. Jamie nodded to the new desk clerk and stepped out into the day.

Elias had phoned earlier, asking him to breakfast. The waiter pulled out the table and Jamie sat on the cushiony green leather chair. From the menu he ordered "Skillet potatoes, wood lawn mushrooms, yellow tortillas, oatmeal, with pippin apples and China cinnamon." The coffee and cream were served in white china, while the freshly squeezed orange juice came frothy in a tall cylinder. The mineral water came in a tulip shaped glass. As Jamie rolled a yellow tortilla Elias gave him his first payment.

"I feel I've been chosen for something important," Jamie said.

"Of course you have."

"Why me?"

"Your dreams have intersected with mine and those of the emissaries."

Jamie recognized that deep in his earliest memory there had been a prelude to all of this. He knew it had always been much more than just a regular dream.

Sitting on the edge of his bed Jamie watched the infrequent mail slide under the door: in this case one envelope, postmarked Thailand. It was from Eric, another cab driver who had gone there to photograph and videotape the bar girls of Pattaya.

Through the blinds Jamie watched the familiar scene of beggars, scavengers and petty criminals. A man in a dumpster, a rag tied around his head, wrestled knee deep in wire. In a doorway two black men and a skinny white prostitute smoked crack. One of the men did a chicken dance after his hits. An elderly Chinese woman went through a trash can with a coat hanger. A wreck of a man sat on the curb and looked at nothing. The man in the dumpster moved on, his shopping cart loaded with gray and black coils of wire as though he now carried the head of some urban giantess. He steered the load expertly down the street.

* * * * *

The Chief, looking like a character from an old Dick Tracy episode, stood by the window and stared out at the city. He sat back at his desk and scanned a report. On his phone a red light blinked off and on. It reminded him of a mindless cyclops.

"Send them in," a weariness was evident in his voice.

Two heavy-set detectives in ill-fitted suits trudged in, one carrying a styrofoam cup of coffee. The Chief gestured them to seats. The heavier of the two spoke.

"Chief, we had Elias, we had him cold." He shook his head. "We threw him in the van. We turned a corner and damn it if the van's not behind us. We circled back and there 'tis parked. Chief, I'm sorry to report we found two dead patrolmen."

He held up two fingers as though his boss was a moron.

"Elias was long gone."

The detective shrugged and looked around the room. The Chief remained silent and eyed the other one who was finishing off his coffee with a slurping sound. The Chief glared at him until he reached over and daintily dropped it in the trash. The Chief was the overseer of field agents. The Committee had sent him to San Francisco after receiving reports that Elias was there. How could a sixty-six year old man continue to evade them with such finesse and vitality? The Chief scratched his head. He would give it another week before returning to Committee headquarters in Washington D. C.

* * * * * *

Elias stepped out of his robe and, naked, squatted until his buttocks almost touched the floor. He placed his palms under his chin and closed his eyes. He again saw his arrival to this time, when he'd discovered Winks, a babbling soul left for dead after an almost fatal beating by a gang of wharf thugs. Elias had nursed him, fed him and healed him. Winks had been at his side ever since.

Elias saw an explosion of stars and glimpses of lost Lemuria, the island that was Eden. But then the wars came and the telepathic Cyclops arrived by the thousands on rafts from the world of caves. At the same time the Great Chaos hit and the world broke apart.

On an empty beach the emissaries appeared. They presented the first flash; he was one of the select and would survive. Elias opened his eyes and flushed a deep red.

Discordant sound seeped out of a cracked window three stories up, becoming infectious and haunting. Under a street lamp two figures stood just out of where the light died.

"You're a good stall Winks," Elias said, back in his three piece suit. "Just don't wait so goddamn long. Watch my signal then go."

Winks shook his head.

"Watch me and go. You do a nice job once you move."

Wink's mouth made an attempt at a smile. His jacket

Part One

clashed frightfully with his slacks and this worked to his advantage as a stall, his ungainliness and distracting pattern combinations setting people a little off balance.

"Papers?" Elias asked.

Winks patted his pocket.

"Remember. One pull the paper drop. Two pulls the bump. Three the fit. Four mustard. Five the antique bottle. Six you're drunk."

Winks nodded.

"I got it boss." He repeated the code singsong.

Elias looked askance, frowned.

They walked off separately but a few moments later both arrived at a busy square. Flower booths, shoe shine stands, cafes and bars were all doing business. Streetcars were boarded while other passengers were getting off. Elias sat on a bench; Winks bobbed back and forth twenty feet away. Then Elias spotted a hit: a young male wearing glasses and carrying an expensive camera and a leather case. He had the wide-eyed look of a tourist.

Elias rubbed his brow and pulled his earlobe once. Winks sprang into action. In a moment he was in front of the young man dropping a handful of papers. Winks loudly and piteously began to bawl. Touched, the boy sat his equipment down to help him. Elias moved with the quickness of a shadow and by the time the young tourist realized what had happened, Winks had also disappeared into the landscape.

A bus station locker area. Elias spotted an older man in a bright green suit who looked hung over. He was carefully and painfully trying to read the locker instructions. Elias was about to move but something stopped him: police shoes, the plant had not changed his shoes. Elias walked away.

Elias had Winks staggering about on a fake drunk which would culminate in a fit: false teeth ajar, howling and jerking about on the ground. A crowd would gather and gasp and gawk. Moving through the crowd Elias would skillfully lift a wallet here or even cut a purse from an old lady's arm there. Pages of the day's already forgotten newspaper blew down the dirty street.

At Jamie's hotel two men leaned against a wall. They wore white shirts and stripped ties under their suits. One was black, the other white, but both had dull, sunken eyes. Right away he knew they were not waiting to check in. They stepped into the street and moved towards him purposefully. He walked away fast, then ran for a cab stopped at a red light. He caught it just in time.

The driver, an older black man, stepped on the gas. Jamie

PORTS OF HELL

looked back at their angry faces. He was wanted for something.

Jamie directed the driver past a block of tall lemon colored buildings, a park and a neighborhood of white-and-honey colored houses with tall gables and balconies that extended over elaborate gardens.

Past an iron gate and a wooded area stood an elegant three-story Victorian. It was the address Elias had previously given him. Jamie told the driver to pull over.

He rang the bell and waited. The sun was setting, transforming the trees to dark gold. Winks let him in and they rode a small elevator to the third floor. Tall windows overlooked the bay where clouds were moving in.

A few days later with Winks, Jamie did a quick checkout at his hotel. He put a call into the cab company. The dispatcher wanted to know if he was at the same address. Jamie found that suspicious. He said yes and hung up.

One evening, as Jamie was strolling the grounds, he heard a sound and stepped back behind a tree. At a clearing Elias appeared. The greenery around him rustled from a steady night wind; a pulsing red light zoomed towards Jamie, just over his head. Elias walked towards him smiling.

Anna returned to the city. By phone they arranged a time and a place to meet. Jamie spotted her from a distance. They embraced in the light rain and held each other a while before walking on. She was rejuvenated after her stay at a clinic in Calistoga: that town of the healing hot springs. The clinic had overlooked a glider airfield and she had found the take offs and landings as therapeutic as any of the massages, mud baths or acupuncture sessions she had endured. Jamie asked about the stabbing and she laughed. He loved her laugh.

"He was a Committee stooge, Jamie. Now shall we have a rich meal? I've had all the health drinks I can stand."

They choose a table by a window with lace curtains. It had stopped raining and the streets looked enchanted. Everything was outlined with a glow and there were lamps suspended above like huge goldfish bowls. Jamie asked her what she knew about the Committee.

"Darling, you must get your instructions and information from Elias. He's the liaison with the emissaries."

Anna refused to discuss it anymore. She held a piece of poached salmon, as pink as mango ice cream to his mouth. She had a voracious appetite and finished off half of his T-bone steak as well as a salad that had

Part One

appeared mysteriously sometime during the meal. Over dessert and coffee Anna's shoeless foot moved up Jamie's leg and rested on his crotch.

After dinner they walked to a theater that was nearby. Although it was closed Anna produced a key. In the near dark they stepped onto a stage where some large cushions were strewn. "Could you put this uniform on please?" Anna pleaded. Jamie dutifully changed into the Army uniform she had produced. She began licking and kissing his penis to the point that Jamie felt like he was losing his mind. In the dim light she unfastened her skirt to reveal that she was wearing no undergarments. He stuck his finger into her mouth and she sucked it. She pleaded for him to stick his penis up her arse and produced a jar of Vaseline. "I'm just a walking cunt tonight!" Anna said. "How do you like my ass?" she asked. "I love your ass," Jamie said thickly. "Moan when you fuck me please!" Jamie returned her caresses and kissed her everywhere he could as they made love. Did her vaginal muscles convulse in a seemingly endless orgasm or was that him? It was such a rush of pleasure he couldn't be sure. Afterwards, relaxed, looking at each other, they became aware that they were not alone. The air had become frosty.

Elias stepped forward and Jamie felt he was standing at the edge of the universe: the stars and the red lines of space dissolving before him.

Elias, Anna and Jamie sat on a bench in Huntington Park. Elias shared two photographs. Jamie remembered Elias had taken them on his first visit to the suite. In the first, Jamie was holding a drink with an almost startled expression. In the second he looked as though he was dissolving into a shadow. The dark sedan pulled up and Elias headed towards it. Jamie felt especially sharp and stirring with a new energy.

Across the street at a side entrance to a restaurant a waiter smoked a cigarette. His loud tie was tucked into the breast pocket of his white shirt.

"Committee or not?" Anna asked.

"Not."

A nearby gardener, watering some shrubs, took a quick drink from the hose.

"And him?" she asked.

"Again no." A cab pulled up. The driver had his cap pushed back; the dispatcher's rattle coming from his radio. Jamie wasn't sure. Anna whispered that he was not Committee and therefore safe to take.

They traveled around the city for hours; Jamie identified one

PORTS OF HELL

Committee agent. One giveaway Anna pointed out was their sunken, drug addict-like eyes: another was a tattoo of an eye within a square usually on the arm.

Elias sat behind a huge desk. Anna and Jamie sat across the room. A red glow emanated from Elias' eyes. He stood, took off his robe and, naked, approached a full-length mirror. He made a circle in the air. The red glow seeped into the mirror. A red light replica of Elias formed and looked out at them.

Later, in bed with Anna, Jamie nuzzled her bare back. She turned and covered his eyes with her hands. He plunged back into a dream. A red glow of himself formed in a mirror. A red disk moved across the evening sky.

Elias appeared at the foot of the bed in a yellow vapor. He spoke to someone Jamie could not see.

"Again fascinated with dreams and shadows as a child."

At Anna's building, there was no door guard present so Jamie took the elevator and let himself in. Just up from a nap, she sat sleepily at the edge of the bed. He knelt and began to undress her. Her hands moved over his neck and shoulders.

"I've been thinking about fucking you all day," he said. Anna suddenly slapped his face. Then she laughed crazily. Angry and aroused all at once Jamie pinned her to the bed.

"Do you want to watch me pee?" she asked. But then she began begging him to let her up and when he did she moved away to the vanity mirror. She began to paint her eyes. Once she had transformed her visage into something like a Vegas show girl she came back and began biting on his ears. "I could tie you up and fuck with your head," she cooed. Jamie pressed his tongue to a nipple.

"You do that nicely," she murmured and laid back, propping a pretty leg on his shoulder.

At the bar, across from Anna's building, Jamie was greeted by a graceful Asian lady who smiled and brought him a drink. There was a flutter of recognition in her dark eyes. The place had mirrors on the walls which made it seem larger. A pinball machine appeared to be in its own little room until his eyes adjusted. The ceiling was lined with colored balloons, left up from some special occasion. Anna arrived, sat on a stool and gave him a juicy kiss. The Asian girl brought her a glass of red wine and caressed her hand quickly as she set it down.

Anna warned Jamie that he must be on guard: it seemed the Committee had a warrant out. Anna had a peculiar charm act-

Part One

ing childlike and naive when she wanted, or wise and experienced at other times. She told him she was inspired by what she had become a part of: it reminded her of the fables and stories of witchcraft on which she had nourished her mind as a young girl.

The only other patrons at the bar were two matronly women who nursed their drinks. A TV showed an interview with Dr. Hunter, but when Jamie finally got the bartender to turn it up it was over. Jamie finished his drink, and signaled the bartender for a refill. Steam rose from the coffee and hot water pots and Jamie's mind also drifted somewhere above him. Someone sat down beside him, a biker type with stringy wet hair. He thumped Jamie's arm, bringing him back to Earth. The biker was wearing much-too-small blue sunglasses.

"Hey, d'you think these fit?"

Jamie didn't answer and the biker didn't wait for one. Jamie was afraid he could be Committee.

"Somebody gave 'em to me," the biker said.

"They look fine," Jamie lied.

"I always liked blue," the biker added but then slumped into a brooding silence. Anna sensed Jamie's apprehension and reassured him by breathing in his ear and placing her hand on his thigh.

The paper was there on the bar top. Jamie scanned the headline story. A well armed man had killed eight and injured six people at a law office in a downtown high-rise. The gunman had then placed a .45 under his chin and pulled the trigger one last time. The photo of the man revealed the hollow eyes of a Committee agent. Jamie paid the bill and they left.

Anna had had too many glasses of wine and vamped around the crowded apartment like a depraved exotic dancer. He heard her flush the toilet, knock something over and then she was there, on top of him. They stayed like that for a while before he rolled her over. Her body twisted, writhed and pushed up violently. Then she smiled lazily, sat up glassy eyed and looked at her breasts as if to review them for any errant blemishes. He whispered to her but she did not respond. Her breathing however picked out a rhythm congruent with his amorousness. He felt her dowsing fingers tracing the surfaces of his genitalia. He found her mouth. "Oh-h-h Jesus," Anna gasped when he mounted her with the crazed look of a satyr.

Elias called, giving Jamie a time and date to see him. Three days later, in the wan light of early morning, Winks let him into the suite. As if dealing Jamie a

PORTS OF HELL

hand of poker Elias set out an airline ticket, money, two credit cards and a passport. It was Jamie in the photo but the name read "David Kuhns." Elias played with a flamboyantly flowered tie clipped to his shirt that came down a few inches past his belt.

"You're off to Koh Samui, a quote, paradise island in the gulf of southern Thailand."

Already Jamie felt his excitement mounting. Elias sipped a glass of juice, made a little monkey sound of pleasure and set it down.

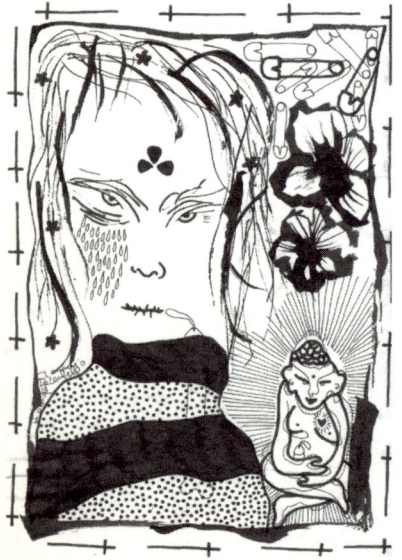

"Your cover is a travel writer."
"I have some questions," Jamie said, wondering where to start.

Elias made a violent gesture, as though trying to force the air in front of him to solidify so he could mold it into something else. He gestured to the ceiling.

"Answers come in different times, Jamie. It's time to go. The Committee is moving in."

Jamie's memory seemed to vanish. A distant, inner voice instructed him to step up and face himself and this world he had entered.

Last night in town, he walked with Anna down to the bay and over to Fort Mason. They found a remote spot, leaned against a tree and watched the container ships moving across the bay. A warm wind massaged them and birds flew overhead. Patterns of light formed and danced across the water. They held each other tightly but for the rest of the evening avoided each other.

Anna took enough Valium to drug herself to sleep. Yes, he would miss her. Yes, he would miss falling into bed with her but much more than that. He would miss minute and insignificant things about her. He wished she was coming but he was instructed to go to Thailand alone. Feeling the unavoidable sadness he quietly left the apartment.

Part One

THAILAND

At the Bangkok airport Jamie collected his bags and changed dollars for baht: eight by fifteen inch red-and-purple bills with the King on the front. He found a cab and struck a deal. Two hours later in a state of combined stimulation and fatigue he was dropped at an outdoor bar in the musky animal air of Pattaya. Pattaya, he read was the notorious sex playground for mostly farang (Western) males, rivaled only by Bangkok's Patpong Road and the island of Phuket. At night the place was dusty and pungent. He took a seat and ordered a Mekong whiskey soda. A boy strolled by with a boa constrictor wrapped around him and carrying a Polaroid camera. He was on the lookout for indulgent tourists. Someone stepped up and sat down. It was Eric.

"You finally made it Jamie."

"Yes and I still feel like I'm flying."

Eric was a few years older, had deep set brown eyes and a thin hungry look. An adventurer who had worked on a schooner in the Caribbean, smuggled marijuana out of Mexico in a high speed car and had some dealings in the gem trade in Burma. Lately he'd been dealing in Thai porn, which allowed him to earn enough money to take side trips to Cambodia and Vietnam.

Jamie had met him when they were both driving cab in San Francisco. Eric had filled Jamie's head with lurid and romantic tales of Southeast Asia. Eric gestured across the street to an open bar where Thai girls cavorted with some elderly white men. The girls were both coy and seductive, while the gents seesawed between lasciviousness and boredom.

"Old ladies as far as they're concerned," Eric explained. "That's for public display and to keep the police happy. Behind closed doors the girls are much younger. Too young, in some cases."

Jamie noticed that not everyone was interested in the Thai bar girls. Some men went with boys, others with the katoeys who looked like girls and were referred to as "lady boys". Jamie and Eric drank, talked and watched the sidewalk traffic move through the go-go night of Pattaya. A Thai bar girl sat next to Jamie, put her head on his shoulder and held his arm. Eric asked if he was interested. Jamie found her sad eyes and frailty anything but sexy. He said no. Eric said something in Thai and Jamie was relieved when she disengaged and drifted away.

Eric pointed out some of the local characters. "Here comes old

PORTS OF HELL

Pete, he's seventy-eight and still chasing young tail. He has to inject some shit into his dick to get it hard. One night he was with this cute little babe and when he wanted to fuck her he went to the bathroom to take his shot. But she came in and caught him and freaked out."

Old Pete said hello and ordered a drink. "See that ugly guy?" Eric gestured towards a guy with a sullen, demented look on his round face.

"We call him the Golem."

The Golem sidled through the crowd, glanced over his shoulder and ducked into a bar that looked like a giant pineapple.

"He creeps everybody out," Eric said with distaste. "The girls are never young enough for him."

Other friends of Eric's stopped by and compared notes on which clubs currently had the best girls. They discussed the girls as race horse fanciers might discuss prize thoroughbreds. Then the talk shifted to "feminism" and their shared hatred of it.

Old Pete seemed to drift off as he spoke nostalgically of Honolulu when it had been a wide open bachelor's paradise.

"They're mostly hard-core players," Eric explained after they had left. "Here for the shows but are headed for the brothels inland, where the girls are near perfect and lighter skinned." He took a sip of his drink.

"You know, for all the nonstop sex the girls are fairly innocent, very polite and clean, not like your American pros. They'll go with you for 'long time' or 'short time'. Long time could entail making you breakfast and cleaning up your place and the nice girls always wai you before they leave."

He imitated the "wai" gesture placing praying hands under his chin. He gave a slight bow.

"Respect's important. The Buddhist philosophy is tolerance and I relate to it more than any Western religion."

Eric spoke Thai with the bartender and arranged for Jamie to leave his bag with him.

A mask wearing, one armed mannequin rode one of the silver elephants that flanked the entrance to a disco they passed. A cute Thai girl fell in between them and Eric introduced her as Nan. She smiled and proudly presented Jamie with a semi-official looking laminated card that read, "HIV negative". Jamie acknowledged that he was impressed, not knowing really how to respond. She laughed and smiled at them both. Eric said he was looking out for her since her Swedish boyfriend was back home.

"I fuck her of course. She's a

Part One

whore but a nice kid. She likes me even though I'm a cheap charlie."

"Yea you cheap charlie," Nan laughed.

She said something in Thai and Eric translated noncommittally.

"She says she likes you. Do you want her?"

"Another time," Jamie said, again not knowing the proper etiquette. He wondered if everybody he was to meet would be offering themselves. Eric told her that Jamie already had a girlfriend. She giggled and said something in Thai.

They made their way down to the beach, past the ghostly wrecks of some old ships. Eric pointed out a house made entirely out of roots. They sat and talked under the soft hazy lights along the esplanade. Eric translated abbreviated versions for Nan, who kicked at the sand like an anxious school girl. On the way back they stopped at another club where Eric was known. Over drinks, they watched a group of slender, semi-nude Thai girls dance with little enthusiasm to a disco beat. The dancers seemed to mirror Jamie's own mood. The long trip had finally hit him. He needed to get some sleep.

There was a vacancy at a notorious hotel where a heroin bust had just occurred. Jamie checked in but the insane singing of Carpenters songs at the karaoke bar across the street kept him up most of the night.

The following day he sat with Eric in a bar on a busy street. A line of motorbikes were parked in front. A different smell in the day time, he thought, more of pollution. There was a water mark on the table and Eric made a circle using his finger. "Yes, I'm with Elias too," he said grinning. This confirmed Jamie's theory. Eric walked him to the bus station and watched him board. He told Jamie a bit about Koh Samui and various ways to get there. He advised him to look up someone named Toon.

The streets of Bangkok were full of revelry for the King's birthday. After Jamie found the train station he asked the ticket seller how long the celebration would last. The man gave him three different answers: three days, five days, one week. Jamie boarded the train for Surat Thani, the province that Koh Samui was in. He was shown to a window seat next to a hippie with dreadlocks and a gaggle of bead necklaces. Jamie stashed his bag overhead and eased past the hippie. An almost overpowering odor of stale perspiration hung in the train but dissipated as they pulled out.

The hippie was from Australia and had a job waiting for him on

PORTS OF HELL

Koh Tao as a diving instructor. He was currently frustrated with his girlfriend because she had a heroin problem. In a month she would be getting out of the detoxification center and joining him. He would work for six months then go on to Egypt. The Aussie had brought along a bag of cassettes and showed Jamie his collection of heavy metal tapes. Jamie asked him if he had heard of the Saints. He hadn't. When he caught Jamie looking at a silver goat's head that hung from his neck he clutched it.

"I'm not into Satan or anything. I don't do rituals or any of that. I just like the way it looks." But wasn't his diving in these exotic locales a ritual of sorts that enabled him to travel through the aquatic underworld? Jamie pondered this for a moment.

He asked Jamie where he was going and what he did. Jamie said he was a travel writer but that he had come to Thailand to write a science fiction novel. He said he was working on it at that very moment. The hippie smiled widely and patted another case at his feet.

"All science fiction, mate. I've a wild imagination and can't read anything else."

He mentioned different authors and books but, not being much of a sci-fi reader, Jamie didn't say much. The hippie put his headphones on and looked content. Occasionally he would mutter something or play air guitar. During the night Jamie awoke, shivering. The air conditioning was on full throttle. A red light, left over from a dream, appeared in his mind's eye. It seemed to spread through him and warm him; soon he was back asleep.

Early in the golden morning they transferred to a bus somewhere in Surat Thani. They traveled a few more miles on jungle dirt roads before they arrived at a pier where an old ferry was moored. They were offered breakfast by some children in a lone hut.

The Australian ate two platefuls of scrambled eggs, toast and two bananas. Jamie passed on the food and instead had a smoke and looked out at the water. Afterwards he headed towards the ferry. Down below deck he found a seat.

The sea, which had been almost eerily calm, now churned and heaved. Before long the passengers, mostly Thais and a few backpackers, began to display various degrees of sickness. One girl began minor regurgitation almost delicately into her handkerchief. The Australian leaned over and vomited loudly. Although Jamie felt queasy, he

Part One

went on deck and the air helped to soothe him. For the next hour the ferry was tossed on the sea like some insignificant toy; then the waters magically calmed and they headed in to dock at Koh Samui. A little wobbly, Jamie walked the long pier to the street and boarded one of the little truck taxis called songtaews.

An hour later he arrived on the other side of the island. Jamie climbed down from the songtaew and headed through a field of tall weeds on a beaten path the driver had pointed out. The path led to a white beach, by tall palms and emerald green water. He watched the sea change to a clear sparkling blue and gradually turn inky at the horizon under the wide tropical sky. A Thai boy juggled mangoes, two pretty girls sat in shallow water and a spaced out hippie with a gibbon on his shoulder walked through the surf. Small green lizards moved quickly about and disappeared. There was a group of raised, white bungalows with thatched roofs. Jamie went to the office and arranged to rent one.

On the beach Jamie waded into the clear water. He spotted a plump gray creature about two feet long resting on the sandy floor. It opened one soft black eye, then shut it, continuing its underwater dreams. Schools of blue fish swam by and Jamie saw a miniature skull. Then another and another. He'd discovered an underwater graveyard of small rocks that resembled skulls. When he was waist deep he dove in. Jamie had arrived at a place that seemed to have been awaiting him and now urged him to continue his part in the story that was unfolding around him.

After a cold shower Jamie studied a map of the island. He wondered what a map of his subconscious would look like. Would it surface on its own someday and dominate his waking hours?

Down a road of mud and puddles Jamie came upon a water buffalo with eyes as old as mythology. It was wallowing and rocking back and forth in a deep pool of a ditch. Its tail swished muddy water across its back and it looked up in its torpor, proudly displaying the horns of a Serapis. In a pond, frogs skipped on the surface and orange carp swam underneath.

After a quick dark rain the sun reappeared with a fury. Birds began to sing and almost at once everything was again dry. Jamie watched the final drops fall from the eaves of his roof. He heard the buzzing of a motorbike in the distance. A temple rooftop was visible through a setting of banana trees and twisting ivy. A simple round bamboo table ringed with matching chairs was set up in the garden next door. Jamie sat at the table and was profoundly soothed by some unearthly sound that seemed to generate from his own mind.

That night he walked past the beach barbecues, the sound was still with him and the red glow too. The moon was partially hidden behind the clouds. Dim lights burned within red-and-white striped lanterns that hung from trees that stretched out over the water. The smell of incense wafted from small shrines. He walked past Thai women who sat on mats and asked "You want ma-sage?"

A wooden sign read: "Long Beach Bar," in dark blue over peeling white paint crawling with ants. Illuminating the sign was a fluorescent cylindrical bulb. Some of the ants had gotten too close and had been zapped dead. Jamie plodded through the sand up to the bar. It was entirely made from bamboo and empty except for a vendor he had seen around. He introduced himself as Toon. Toon had expressive brown eyes, flattish nose, small mouth and large crooked white teeth. He was younger than Jamie, half his height and moved with the grace of a young animal.

They left the bar and walked down to where the beach was flat. Toon squatted almost to the ground, his palms under his chin, fingers on his cheeks. He stayed completely still and looked out to the sea. Jamie tried the posture but found he could not squat as long as him and had to stand and ease the pain out of his legs. But Jamie had felt something happening inside of him. As though his cells had tried to rearrange themselves somehow.

Toon laughed. "You practice every morning."

Toon stood again and fell fluidly back into the position.

"Morning morning morning," he instructed. Then he picked up his things and walked off. The squat posture was a resting position for Asians as well as the standard bathroom posture. And in a magazine Jamie had seen a similar position for praying to Buddha. He felt that if he could master it without pain a connection point would be developed to a Kundalini like vibration. He had watched Elias meditating in this posture and felt it was probably connected to an ancient rite of Lemuria.

A radar closeness was quickly developed with Toon and Jamie would know just when he was going to turn up. Mornings they would sit together under an ample umbrella, drinking coffee while exchanging basic English and Thai conversation lessons. Sometimes they spent the entire day laughing and practicing.

Part One

One muggy afternoon Jamie walked through the jungle, already a lost and weary explorer. He found a paved road which led to a cafe and one of the island's songtaew yards. A half dozen were parked in the dusty lot. In a raised open hut, a shirtless driver was stretched out fast asleep on a wooden pallet. His head rested on a cushion which sat on top of a small wooden block. Inside the cafe Jamie found other drivers reclining on raised wooden beds. One, smoking, sat alone. Two others sat at a table eating. Another leaned against a wall with a feather duster in his hand. They all watched a Kung Fu movie on TV imagining, Jamie mused, a more exciting life on the streets of Hong Kong.

Later that night, at a restaurant on the beach, Jamie noticed the heavily tattooed youths in a far corner almost blending into the woodwork. A waiter wearing a crisp white shirt appeared at Jamie's table with a silver platter of freshly caught squid and king prawns. The seafood was generously laced with garlic and served with a side of pineapple chili sauce and rice and a vegetable Jamie didn't recognize. He ate slowly and savored every bite. When he was done the waiter returned with a finger bowl and hot tea. *"Cha lawn,"* he gestured to the tea.

Jamie felt that the days on Samui were directed by the extraordinary sky and waters. When night came, the feeling that he was living in a dream seemed all the more profound. Jamie felt he was drifting in some idyllic and remote solar system. The heat was tempered by a reliable island breeze. His skin turned brown and from his walks, swims and new diet he dropped ten pounds. He usually wore a bathing suit or shorts, flip flops and in the evenings a shirt.

He practiced the squat position and, after three minutes, an exhilaration would rush through him that would almost topple him. What followed was a trepidation which gave way to an unfolding sharpness of the intellectual process that seemed to push into the unknown. Through a series of reflections full of creation and chaos the sky would turn red and Jamie would fall into a kind of delirium. He would be directed by the red light and pass through a tunnel and arrive in a garden. Stars would explode all around him.

Heavy rains came and the tourists stayed indoors and complained. By a grove of papaya trees full of the still green fruit, Toon motioned and Jamie went into the pavilion. Toon moved about, turning down the rolled-up bamboo screens and leaning the plastic chairs against the tables. When he stepped in the sky roared and the rain came down hard. A falling coconut hit the roof with a bang.

"Coconut bomb," Toon said and laughed, then drifted away, leaving Jamie to his thoughts on that rainy day. Jamie thought about Elias, his other-worldliness, and at the same time, his earthiness. Through the screens he could see a figure moving about in the jungle and for a moment he thought it was Elias. But then he saw that it was an older Thai man with lunar blue eyes.

That night Jamie sat under a colossal orange moon. He was the only one at the outdoor cafe. He was having English tea. The sea was dark and silent. Suddenly the moon become small, pale and surrounded by clouds. Jamie felt he was taking part in an occult ritual. It was as though he was somehow moving the moon with his mind and it was a million years earlier. White foam lapped at the beach where a couple danced. A white albino moth landed on his hand, circled, flew off. Under the gas lit lamp a fly landed in the saucer, doomed to a milky death. During the night something pricked or bit Jamie's neck.

Jamie roamed the dirt road a block behind the beach that was crammed with beer bars, scooter rentals, noodle stands, money exchanges and so on. Jamie went there for the Bangkok Post and other odds and ends. The Post was either one or two days late or didn't come at all. He sat down at a little fly-blown place and had breakfast. He watched the songtaews roar by filled with backpackers headed for the ferries in Nathon: island hoppers headed for Koh Phangan, Koh Tao, or Nang Youn. An entire family of five drove by on a scooter. Jamie felt the bump that had appeared on he neck. He saw a pharmacy across the road that advertised "DOCTOR." An attractive Asian girl in a kimono stood in the doorway in front of all the medicines.

The pretty doctor directed Jamie to a back room and with light fingers examined the bump. She put a Band-Aid on it and handed him a pouch that contained purple pills. She told him to return in three days. Jamie bought some menthol inhalers that some of the islanders used to clear out their noses. It gave a slight lift and some of the locals even became addicted to it. Saucer eyed youngsters would stand by their motorbikes eating ice cream and jamming the inhalers up their noses.

Later that day Jamie sat in a beach cafe and fingered the bump.

Part One

It seemed to be softening or shrinking but he wasn't sure. He reapplied the band aid. On the wall an almost transparent albino lizard with glistening black eyes flicked a pink tongue.

"Would you care to join us? No sense sitting alone," a man who sat with an older woman said to him. Mother and son were traveling Asia together and struck Jamie as characters out of an offbeat travel novel. Jamie wondered if they were Committee. They continually drank coffee and smoked cigarettes. The man was deeply tanned, wore sunglasses and one small gold earring. The woman had short, white hair and looked to be at least eighty except that she had the body of a thirty year old. She had the off-kilter eyes of a crone.

They claimed to be New Zealanders. The son removed his sunglasses and boasted that he was a professional traveler. He jabbered on and on about his adventures. He ended his tale recounting a poor massage he had recently received in Chiang Mia. The mother had peppered his narrative with comments in a thick Germanic accent, having heard it all before. Now she told a story with violent gestures concerning dogs on Fiji. Jamie couldn't follow it. He passed on an invite to go to their bungalow for wine. He decided they were not Committee agents. Mostly a hunch, but they did not have sunken eyes and he had spotted no tattoos of an eye within a square.

Three days later, Jamie returned to the pharmacy. He found the girl doctor barefoot, by the register, wearing another colorful kimono and applying eye shadow. Jamie took a blast of an inhaler and watched her finish up. She saw him watching and smiled. She directed him to the back room again. Incense burned under a framed yellowed photo of some people mystically draped in robes. She looked at the bump with a magnifying glass. She moved across the room, stopped and examined a tray of needles. He had hoped to avoid pain but now, resigned, sat back and searched for some stoicism. He found a crack on the wall to stare at, but out the corner of his eye saw her approaching. She swabbed the boil with something that smelled medicinal, but he felt no freezing or numbing. She examined a needle in the light. Like a fine piece of barbed wire was slowly being pulled and twisted in there the pain arrived and he squirmed, grunted and broke a sweat. Then it was over.

A songtaew took Jamie to Nathon, the main town on the other side of the island. He watched the driver's helper strapping luggage onto the roof. Like most drivers this one crammed in as many people as possible. Once the truck was full, passengers had to stand on the back step and hang on. There were even little plastic child stools kept underneath the seats, which could be scooted out into the narrow aisle so even more people could be loaded in, forced to squat at the other passengers' knees. Some refused this indignity and either found room on the back step or waited for the next one. Jamie knew that the ride took about an hour.

He got off by the piers where the ferries came in. He wondered when he would be contacted by Elias. He had said he was coming to Thailand but was first going to Indonesia. Jamie walked over to a restaurant and took a table. Two sunburned Germans wearing garish beachwear entered noisily. They had glittering, nasty, little eyes. They sat at a table and a Thai boy came by to take their orders.

"Booger" one said. The boy was perplexed.

"Booger booger!" they both spoke loudly.

The boy left and returned with an older boy.

"Booger booger!" shouted the Germans.

The older boy leaned down. "Hamburger?"

"*Ja*. Hambooger!"

A cautionary flag in Jamie's mind unfurled one morning as he spoke with an older man sitting in a deck chair, a folded newspaper on his lap. What hair he had left he wore long and he kept adjusting his glasses. He had a small mean mouth and a small mean way about him. Jamie had a strong hunch he was a Committee man and also of German descent. Sure enough, closer inspection proved that he had sunken eyes and a tattoo of a square with an eye in the middle. It was partially visible on his wrist and he quickly covered it with his sleeve.

He asked what Jamie was doing on Samui. Jamie said he was writing: drifting back and forth between a travel essay and a science fiction story. The old man made a sour expression and seemed stumped for the moment.

Jamie excused himself announcing he was going for a swim. The old man looked at him shrewdly. Jamie floated in a sea as warm as Eden and tried to clear his mind. When he got out, he dried in the sun and resumed reading from a slick magazine from Bangkok. An article about spirit masters had gotten his attention. His chair wasn't far from the old German's bungalow. The old man finally went in and slammed shut his door. Jamie

Part One

made some notes. Things were picking up on Samui.

At a Buddha shrine a white cat ate the offerings. Down the beach a boy crouched and looked at something that resembled a rat. As Jamie got closer he found it was a bloated white fish with no eyes and a pink almost human mouth. The thing was covered with spines.

"Puffa fish," the boy explained, "puff up when frightened."

"But its eyes…"

"Dog ate eyes," the boy laughed. Jamie remembered a show he had seen. The Puffer fishes deadly poison was used in the concoction to make zombies in Haiti.

A loud dog fight in a nearby field distracted Jamie. Toon, who he hadn't seen for a while, came in from the road; aimed and fired his slingshot. There was a yelp and the dogs dispersed. Dog mortality was high due to disease, malnutrition and the "Dog Men" who thinned them out on occasional night raids with clubs. Jamie would see dogs after vicious fights, their flesh raw, digging a hole in the sand to lay in and recuperate. Others he would see dead on the side of the road, covered in dust.

Toon investigated a bad smell coming from behind one of the bungalows and found another dead dog. Its neck and head were smashed, clearly not the result of a fight. It's limp body was hauled away in a wheelbarrow.

Margo, a muscular Dane with dark piercing eyes took the bungalow next to Jamie. He was not Committee, Jamie decided, but there was something off-putting besides the cockiness and sadistic humor of the man. There was some palpable inner tension just below the surface of Margo's defined musculature. This tension gave Jamie an uneasy feeling that, at any moment, Margo might leap into some irrational act. Also unsettling was that his body and head seemed somehow mismatched.

Margo had just visited a katoey friend in Nathon's jail. He told Jamie, who was sitting on his terrace, that the katoey was arrested after a foreigner was robbed after inviting "her" to his bungalow. He said he wanted to try out a "lady boy" and began to act out fucking motions.

"Might be interesting" he winked.

He said that in Denmark he was a policeman, a radioman, but he desired action and Jamie could see his frustration. He tried to release it, it seemed, through sex. Talk always came back to sex: he bragged about his conquests and fantastic orgasms.

Jamie didn't think Margo even

detected that he didn't like him. He was so in love with himself he saw little else. Margo spent the afternoons racing around the island on a motorbike while a sleepy bar girl hung out at his bungalow.

Later Jamie asked Toon what he thought of Margo and without changing his expression he said, "Mi de. No good."

Toon dozed in Jamie's chair. A butterfly flew lazily into a wall then toward the papaya trees.

That night Jamie stood in the darkness and looked out to the sea. A man wearing a striped bath robe, shining a flashlight was coming down the beach. It was the old Committee man. Jamie turned towards him wondering just what he was up to.

"Are you from Germany?" Jamie asked.

The old man glanced around, coughed.

"*Ja.*"

He then began a long monologue in German concerning waterworks somewhere, "waterworks," being the only English word he used. He stopped and asked "waterworks?" and gestured out to the gulf. Jamie shrugged and thought the man insane. Finally he got away from him.

Jamie spent an afternoon searching for a plastic pump for the hefty water bottles he now had delivered, having graduated to "stay long time." In a shop he made pumping gestures. There seemed to be no word for the device. Perhaps waterworks? He laughed to himself. Jamie said the Thai word for water, "nam" and made the pumping gesture again. The shop girl gave him a puzzled look. Then she understood.

"Nathon."

As Toon cleaned out a vacant bungalow he asked Jamie if he wanted anything: a bamboo chair, picture of a waterfall, a chipped mug. Toon opened a magazine to a photograph of the old German and some others waiting for luggage at the Bangkok airport. The article was about airport safety. Jamie tore the page out.

Elias had instructed him to arrange an altar that would serve as a combination totem, fetish and magickal house. Jamie had found a unique piece of cement on the side of the road. There was an open circle at the top and the wider bottom was an open trapezoid. At first he'd used it as a paperweight and showed Toon how it could be used as a bookend. Then he began to sense its power and set it off by itself on the bar of the terrace.

Near a deserted section of the beach Jamie waded in the water and picked up an assortment of

Part One

thin white pebbles that looked like some strange currency; on the beach he found a marooned plastic beetle. He would put the stones in the trapezoid section and the beetle in the circle of his found altar.

From out of the sea Jamie salvaged one of the skull rocks. A misshapen face. A round hole through the head, a barnacle lodged inside. It looked like voodoo, he decided. He would balance it on top of the altar.

The next morning, an agitated Margo showed up at Jamie's terrace to present the wounds that were distributed amongst his arms, legs and head. Some were dressed, others were left open and splotched with a glaring mercurochrome. So began Margo's accident story and with each retelling more was revealed.

Margo was returning from Lamai at night. He was driving a motorbike with only the dimmer, since he was following a car. A Thai boy decided to cross after the lone car had passed and Margo hit him straight on and was thrown from the bike. The islander, who was in bad shape was sent to Surat Thani Hospital on the mainland. But Margo was primarily agitated over the amount of money "they" would want. Paying your way out of the situation was how it was done, he said. Jamie took his exit when Margo began to retell his story to someone else.

Jamie had just gotten his order in at the cafe when, to his chagrin, Margo reappeared. Margo surveyed the place and Jamie half expected some other accident to occur. He retold the story close-up with foul breath. Now conspiratorially he admitted that he had been going too fast. He said that the tourist police were coming in a little while.

"I hate the fucking Thai police," he spat.

Jamie rushed through his breakfast and, when Margo's food arrived, abruptly excused himself.

When evening came Jamie noticed that Margo was still not back from the police station. He walked out to the beach. Hypnotic, almost foreboding sounds came from a bar. He went in and took a seat. Musicians sat on the floor of a shadowy stage: with a variety of drums and a kind of squawking flute. A couple of them chanted along with the rhythm. Three ram Thai dancers with tall golden headgear stepped out from the shadows. When they finished the audience clapped politely.

Jamie decided to try the food but was disappointed. The pineapple juice came thick with added sugar and the shrimp with vegetables contained a long black hair. He wondered if the hair held any occult significance. The waitress looked insulted since he had barely touched the meal. The old German watched from behind a potted plant at the bar.

The following day Margo stopped by Jamie's again to say that after many calls from his "people" and various "important police" including a general in Bangkok the authorities agreed to charge him only three thousand dollars. If the boy died he would have to pay more.

"But if I'm out of here, fuck it," he said and headed off for a shower before catching the ferry.

After this episode Toon began to nail up red-and-white warning signs regarding the slant of the road, driving motorbikes too fast and leaving valuables in boats or at the beach. When he showed up with his hammer and another stack Jamie convinced him that he had put up quite enough.

Jamie's legs had been ravaged by mosquitoes and he had scratched the bites bloody. Toon had given specific instructions not to scratch under any circumstances. Jamie purchased some cans of mosquito spray to give the bungalow a thorough bombing each evening. After that he doused himself with a curiously pleasant repellent and burnt mosquito coils on the terrace.

A tip of gold peaked over the mountains. The stars were smeared across the dark sky. Jamie walked with Elias down a hill and onto the worn steps of a wooden bridge built high on spindly legs. Into the air they sailed, and out over the sea, travelers of another world. Jamie experienced the uncanny feeling of being aware of both the dream and the wakefulness. He watched as the beetle from his altar came to life and made its way to the old German's bungalow. Jamie burned the picture from the magazine and left the ashes where the beetle had been.

After persistent efforts Jamie located a good restaurant on the road: a noodle stand by the kick boxing school served savory, inexpensive dishes. The stand also served as a hangout for old men with broken faces who sipped Coca Cola and took hours to get through the two page newspaper. Jamie discovered that these men had been kick boxers in their youths. At lunch time Jamie watched the students shimmy down poles from thatch roofed huts in the sky and dive into huge bowls of rice and fish doused with hot sauce. The rest of the day they yelled and practiced kicks at weight bags held by others. The ghastly smell of sewage passed by in intervals, stronger on some days than others.

Near the kick boxing school Jamie found a good bakery and

Part One

heard favorable reports about other places. The food served by the beach vendors he always found superb. Toon also sold little fried pies filled with coconut, yam or chicken and intercepted Jamie who was on his way back to his bungalow. Jamie selected three from the neat rows under the cloth in the basket.

"*Sawadee cop*."

"*Sawadee cop*," Toon echoed.

"Special from Bophut for you," he handed Jamie a bag of cannabis. "Two puffs and you are blessed."

The island was thick with marijuana. People passed it freely to him in the little open cafes. Bophut he knew was another beach village, remote and well spoken of. Jamie felt that Samui was so tranquil the days just drifted into each other and time lost some of its tyranny.

One afternoon Jamie found Toon by the front office. He sat at a table absently thumbing through magazines. He and Jamie soon took turns firing slingshots at the poles on the other side of the lot.

Jamie took a keen interest in the slingshot. As a young boy he had never been without one. Toon was impressed with his handling. From that day on Jamie would take a half hour each morning to practice.

One night Jamie stood under a palm tree to the side entrance of a modern hotel. The night was blue, the beach an enchanted esplanade. Some ladies strolled by appearing like dreamy Venuses. Jamie spotted a cat. A sleek orange bobtail had emerged from a garden, most of its face black like a mask. It sauntered over, sniffed and rubbed against him. It crept over to a bucket, its front paws braced on the rim. It looked in and pawed at something. In the bucket was water and at the bottom a dead fish.

The cat watched as Jamie laid the fish on the ground. She bit neatly into it. After her meal she left to explore underneath a temporary stage. Her green eyes flashed as she prowled around. Pale moon deep in the sky. The last full moon was orange and enormous. Jamie remembered wading in the clear water lit by a flood lamp. Out a ways two boys fished with throw nets and a styrofoam box floated in-between them.

One afternoon Jamie found an ice cream vendor scooping up an order from the back of his scooter. It turned out to be a piece of bread with two scoops of sticky rice, coconut ice cream, peanuts sprinkled on top. Under a palm tree Jamie ate the ice cream sandwich and watched as two magnificent elephants with boys atop them came down the main road

PORTS OF HELL

from town.

In the evening Toon came around to find Jamie gazing at his altar. Toon had brought a bowl of sea snails and a plate of sliced limes. They were opened, waiting to be sucked up and eaten. Jamie lifted one, made a face and squeezed lime on it. Expressionless he chewed. Toon was already a little drunk. A cockroach crawled across the table and Toon grabbed a salt shaker and crushed. He laughed dementedly as its tiny legs moved desperately. Toon lifted the salt shaker and swatted the roach away. Jamie gave him a shove.

Restless, Jamie started his morning walk down a road he had not yet explored. After a mile it turned to dirt and he passed through a jungle and came to a small village. Thai pop was coming from a radio somewhere. The locals eyed him casually. Feeling that perhaps he was intruding Jamie walked off on another road which led away from the village. A songtaew was passing up ahead. He called out, waved and it stopped. An hour later he was in Nathon.

In a store Jamie found a water pump and bought a tube of toothpaste which had an illustration of a white man wearing a top hat and a gleaming smile. With a little haggling he bought a pair of jungle print shorts that he came to hate and would later give away. He bought a metal holder for the mosquito incense coils.

Jamie crossed the street looking at a stout woman in the back of an old truck packed high with garlic; the jaws of some tremendous fish tied to the handlebars of a parked bicycle.

At a pharmacy an old man deftly made packets out of newspaper and fastened rubber bands around them. The old man nodded and gestured towards a door in the back. Jamie stepped into a maze of passageways. He followed one to spiral stone steps; at the top he found a white room. In the back were stacks of dark bowls on low tables. A boy knelt and poured hot water on the floor. The steam in the air effected the light and made him feel he had stepped into a carefully planned photograph. The boy smiled and gestured to an ornate doorway. Jamie stepped through a beaded curtain and found himself in a shop filled with ancient maps, swords, knives, amulets, rings and old coins. Behind a case sat a Thai man wearing a silver bar through his columella.

He started: "*Pom mi kong sam rap coon.*" "I have something for you."

"*Cop coon cop.*" "Thank you."

"*Mi pen rai cop.*" "Don't mention it."

The man produced a round

Part One

amulet of dull silver with a speck of Burmese ruby in its center. He threaded a leather string through the hole and fastened it around Jamie's neck.

"Choke de mak mak." "Best of luck."

He nodded towards another door. They wai-ed each other.

At breakfast Toon admired his amulet. He poured canned milk into the coffee and insisted he feed Jamie his first sip. Later Jamie caught a glimpse of Toon as he moved in-between the bungalows in a tall, orange, paper hat left over from some birthday party. The white cat climbed a palm tree to scratch on one of the already faded warning signs.

A gang from Cyprus arrived and rented out three bungalows. They were loud, boisterous and sang along with the tapes they had played at the cafe, toasting Cyprus and getting stupid drunk. The next day, hung over, in black moods, they erected a volleyball net and put Cypriot flags at the top of each pole. The old German had disappeared.

There was an invasion of tourists for the holidays, but it was only for one week and Jamie was secretly thrilled. The mostly European women went topless, wore thongs and paraded about shamelessly. Cat-like Thai women avoided the sun. *"Sangdad roan mak. Mi de,"* they'd say with emphasis: "The sun is very hot, no good." They would only enter the water after the sun had gone down and even then would wear shirts and long skirts. The division between the two types of women was great, yet Jamie felt it was two sides of a very lovely feminine coin.

A beautiful Thai girl walked by Jamie with colorful intertwined ribbons and flower necklaces for Buddha. He caught up with her and started to talk with her. The girl's name was Sunisia. She had dark eyes, long black hair and a big smile. She possessed such a relaxed sensuality it immediately put him at ease. Regardless of the language limitations, he got to know her better. She was something of a teenager but he did not underestimate her: in fact, her juvenile directness was refreshing yet at times disarming.

Sunisa began to spend some nights at Jamie's bungalow.

On one of those nights she was dancing wildly to a tape of Thai pop, giving him warm, seductive looks. When the tape ended she turned pouty, picked up her fan and began to fan her neck.

She looked off into space. Jamie knelt before her and she fell back on the bed giggling. She pushed him away with her feet. He kissed them, cramming her toes into his mouth. She stroked his face and pulled at his ears and murmured Thai love words. Sunisa slipped Jamie's trunks off. She frantically used her tongue, circling the glans of his erect penis. Then her hot mouth clamped onto it. But then she eased off and looked up at him smiling. As they began to make love she tried to reach over to turn off the lamp. Jamie finally let her.

The following day he was stricken with a persistent cough. He tried some medicinal lemon lozenges, a sweet Codeine syrup and orange powdered packets that fizzled into instant droughts; the cough only got worse. Sunisa brought him a container of balm and chastised him for getting sick. As she applied the balm, the cough disappeared. On the beach that evening, watching the sunset, Jamie held Sunisa's hand and felt its contours. He caressed and kissed it. She sighed heavily and fell into him.

In the afternoons Jamie played paddle ball with Toon using the set the Cypriotes had left behind. The cafe had never quite recovered from their stay. Most of the help had quit. Sometimes Jamie breakfasted there and would see that the empty wine and liquor bottles still remained, as did the broken chairs and pieces of the balustrade. The volleyball poles minus net and flags stood as one more reminder to the surviving crew. Jamie continued his dawn regimen of slingshot practice, then the squat position from a hilltop facing the sea. Then he calmed himself with a walk and a swim.

During one of the island's dramatic sunrises Jamie sat with two hipster farangs and their gibbon. Unlike other gibbons this one, named Mong, remained perfectly still on one of the laps and listened to the conversation. They shared a joint and invited Jamie to visit their place, the Moonbar, for a party.

Chat was Welsh, with big brown eyes, a shaved head and one ear pierced countless times. He displayed a slight mania that the gibbon seemed to calm.

English Matt had green eyes, long blond hair and silver braces on his teeth. He was a bit morose and referred to the rest of the world as if Armageddon had already occurred.

Both wore amulets of blue coral in a silver box. English Matt looked closely at Jamie's and made an appreciative sound. Jamie remembered that amulets predated Buddhism. Amulets were worn in Lemuria.

Toon and Jamie set out the night of the party. A passing monsoon whipped the island with intermittent winds and rain, and they had neglected to bring um-

Part One

brellas and had to duck under an open thatched roof. A young Thai boy joined them and they spoke the usual greetings and goodwill.
"*Sawadee cop.*"
"*Coon sabi de mi cop?*"
"*Sabi de cop.*"
The boy offered cigarettes. Jamie realized he hadn't had one in a long time—and he didn't really want one.
"*Mi ow cop coon cop.*"
The rain stopped. They said good-bye and went off in different directions.

On the palm lined road that led to town, a battered taxi pulled over for them. They drove through the streets, through the deep puddles. The driver blew his horn at people and animals; they moved out of the way at the last possible second. On a back road the taxi droned to a stop, sputtered, then started again.

The driver pointed to a spindly-legged bridge built over a reedy swamp. Ritual drumming was carried across the water. Torches lit the way to the other side, where the three connecting huts of the Moonbar stood. At the main hut soundless TVs flickered light on the stoned patrons who perched here and there. In the air rode the heady fragrances of Thai stick, coconut curry and spilled Mekong whiskey. Matt and Chat were at the entrance. Two Thai policemen sat at an outside table drinking Singha Gold.

"No hassle here on the island," Matt said as he came over, his breath reeking of whiskey. He gestured back to the police. "They're well paid."

On the back terrace of the Moonbar the surrounding jungle seemed to seep into Jamie's mind. A dim red light pulsed there too and he felt himself going into a trance. Across the way, two Thais in the costumes of ancient Siam stood like statues. They wore mad mysterious smiles. Then they were gone, particles disappearing. For a short time the moon was obscured by dark clouds but the island came quickly back to life from beams of flashlights that moved cryptically through the jungles and over the beaches.

In the morning Jamie walked along the beach. By some small wooden benches painted pale yellow, an old Thai man had raked leaves and other debris into piles. A faded green-and-orange fishing boat lay on its side. A bearded, middle-aged man was being strapped into a para-sailing harness. The chute spread out behind him like some sinister sky cloak. He grinned idiotically and his girlfriend took a picture. A whistle blew and she shrieked as he was lifted into the air. Vendors walked the beach with sagging shoulder poles on their endless rounds: some carried a small stove at one end and a basket of chicken or corn-on-the-cob on the other, some had their baskets loaded with drinks and fruits.

The monsoon had sent most of the tourists packing. The few who'd remained huddled in restaurants, complaining amongst themselves and peering out at the palms that bent and blew violently.

Jamie patrolled the abandoned tourist areas after his morning regimen. Again he wondered when Elias would contact him and how long he was to stay. He ate a papaya every morning and swam alone in the choppy gray sea. He stood in the churning water and watched wooden planks and debris from sunken boats wash ashore. He studied two small buildings that had collapsed and in their place was a beached tour boat. The mushroom shades that had once lined the area had long since blown away.

The tide covered the beach and ran under the bungalows' raised foundations. The previous day two fishermen had drowned when their boat had capsized. The next day the monsoon was gone.

The morning sun light was reflected from thousands of points on the water. Jamie decided to walk beyond where he had ventured before.

He crossed a wooden bridge that passed over an inlet where fishing boats were tied; on the other side there were bungalows designed like Thai temples. A boy with a wooden cart full of leaves stabbed a pointed stick at more leaves in the sand. There were two fish, hung from a cord strung between two poles. The boy who guarded them explained one was a barracuda and the other a yellow queen fish.

Jamie lost track of time as he walked the long stretches of empty beach. Eventually he approached a monolith of gray boulders which held back the waves.

Behind the boulders he found crude steps that led to the top. The lusty sea rushed in and smashed over the lower rocks, leaving behind inlets and still grottos where submerged crabs sat contentedly. The boulders stretched onward as far as the eye could see. He climbed and hiked them for another hour. Some stubborn demon drove him on and on.

From one spot to another he moved, alternately cautious and daring. He edged by deep chasms, figuring the obstacles had to end sometime. At several points he almost gave up. After he had skirted a ravine or climbed a precipice he would look back at a now treacherous sea breaking over the rocks. Instead of beauty,

Part One

he now saw only danger, a broken or sprained limb at the least.

He came to a spot where the only way past was to jump about ten feet. The drop was three times that onto a bed of jagged rocks. He felt he could not turn back. He had passed some unnamed boundary point. "Jump." Elias' voice resonated in his head.

Once he had stepped back as far as he could, he coiled, ran and leapt. His heart pounded as he nearly crashed on the other side. The urge to defecate came over him and he pulled down his shorts and squatted Thai style.

Jamie looked around and it was as though he had been standing still, or the landscape had magically moved and had placed him back at some earlier spot. Were occult powers at work? Jamie slipped but caught himself from a bad fall, just scraping up his hand.

He reached another peak and there, before him, was an awe-inspiring sight: a seemingly endless terrain of tall and massive rough hewn rocks. Jamie felt he must now try and make his way inland, up an incline of thick jungle which would eventually take him to a road. He was thinking about this when he heard a motor. The boat pulled into view and idled there and the shirtless pilot looked at him hatefully. It was the German Committee man.

Jamie, feeling that he would pull a gun, eyed a boulder to get behind but the old man pulled away and disappeared from sight.

Through the thorny vegetation he plodded, pulling the clinging vines off him as he went. After getting pricked and lashed by various plants, he learned which to avoid. The jungle became denser, however, and wrapped itself around him more relentlessly as he proceeded.

At some spots he had to crawl. A loose sneaker fell off and he had to backtrack to retrieve it.

A butterfly floated by. Then he heard the welcome sound of a car not far away. Jamie continued to climb; he gripped a rock and the top broke off exposing a world of scurrying insect life.

With a final burst of determination, he made it to the summit. He was breathing heavily and shaking slightly. His arms and legs were stripped with bloody lacerations. On the hilltop he sat on a felled tree amongst craggy rocks and ferns, tall grass and white flowers between his legs. Over the tops of some palms was a still sea and another island with a purple hilly area. An insect buzzed his ear and he swatted at it. A bird began to sing a high song from atop a curious tree where clumps of red berries were housed within shriveled purple leaves. The tree looked

PORTS OF HELL

both dead and beautiful.

Jamie closed his eyes and could see the red pulse. When he opened them he saw Elias stepping out from behind a tree. He wore a beige linen suit, white shirt, brown and crème striped tie and a straw hat. He looked around and rearranged his hat.

"Come along," he said. He seemed to part the air with his hands and a path appeared, leading to a bungalow.

In the shower Jamie soaked his head. The cuts had already healed. He joined Elias on the terrace. The night approached and a shadow fell over half of Elias' face. He waved a fly swatter that he referred to as his scepter. Out in the gulf, pinpoints of light shone from ships that had laid anchor. Elias smelled his food thoroughly, then bit in with tiny white teeth. He spoke fondly about a shadow play he had seen in Indonesia. Jamie watched his own shadow, the profile of Elias and that of the constantly moving fly swatter dance on the walls. They too had become a shadow play. Images formed, swelled, multiplied and dissolved.

"Remember shadows," Elias said. "Remember the shadow story as a boy? In India the seers can tell everything about a person from their shadow. As an agent you can become shadow and light."

"The old German Committee man was there today."

"Yes, your training has gone well. You've built your altar and reacquainted yourself with the sling. You've had some progress with shadowing and identification."

"Why isn't the old German gone?"

"You've nothing more to worry about from him."

"And the Committee?"

"Sold out to the Enemy. But they were rotten long before that. They're very strong in America and Europe."

Elias lit a cigarette and looked at Jamie calmly. He made a circle around him with his cigarette. "This is of the highest importance, Jamie. I see you've nicely removed yourself from the world, yet are still in it."

Elias drew an invisible line in the air with his thumb. "We can find the road back to Lemuria and the other worlds." He made another, slower circle around Jamie.

"Time to go," Elias said and handed Jamie an envelope that read 'Bangkok.' He pointed to a path that led back down through the jungle to the beach.

The moon dripped light on the spiral roof of a temple. Jamie entered and followed the sound of chanting from somewhere inside. Shadowy figures moved in the

Part One

deep corners. He passed an old Thai man wearing a wise expression, a peaked cap and a gilded robe. Through a dark, inner chamber he came upon a slender Thai boy on a stage. The boy had pierced his cheeks and tongue with skewers. Around him on pedestals were dishes with eggs cracked open: some contained blood, others rusty nails. Jamie walked through the blue smoke and out into the moist, warm night.

On the beach, lit by a multitude of candles, Thais, in the costumes of ancient Siam, danced silently. Amongst the dancers were the two monks he had passed earlier and the two in costume from the Moonbar.

There was an extraordinary quietness punctuated only by the breaking waves. The sand was like white velvet. Jamie joined in the dance with Sunisa, who appeared by his side. He saw a young girl standing under a fancy pennant of a beetle surrounded by white stones. She held a skull rock cupped in her hands.

The next day Jamie heard the old German was found dead in his bungalow. According to one report, he had been stabbed in the back but the doctor had only found a curious bite mark on his neck. The two Thai policemen, who were really no more then boys, considered Jamie quietly but closely. One briefly looked at his altar, which was no longer occupied.

Mosquito coils burned in the almost still air. It was Jamie's last night on Samui. He scooped out the sweet orange fruit of a papaya with a spoon. Toon's face was talc powdered white and he talked about when he was abandoned as a boy and had lived by his wits for a year in Bangkok's great train station. A man he had met there found him a job at an alligator farm. Later, he landed another job as a runner in Pattaya. It was there that he met Elias, who brought him to Koh Samui.

On his terrace Jamie listened to a car motor's waiting putter then some light hammering on wood. Nearby someone cleared their throat; someone else began to sing then the voice drifted away. Sunisa, in a crimson silk kimono, moved gracefully through the bungalow and lit a small spirit lamp.

She handed Jamie a card with an address in New Zealand. She leaned her arm on his shoulder.

"This card I give my address at New Zealand. You know why I go there? I go there for going to university. I hope you very well with everything. You look this card. Where? Yes, yes New Zealand."

47

PORTS OF HELL

She frowned and stroked the back of his head. She spoke lower. "You forget me already? Oh, I'm sad. I still miss you always. Okay I know you don't forget me. Good. Do you know when I saw you every time? I so happy all the time."

Sunisa smelled of the musky dried flowers she had been working with earlier. Jamie held her close. The tide had receded so far and was so shallow that he could have walked out to another smaller island.

"Finished," Toon said and pointed to the ankle-deep water. They both knew that his stay too was finished and the receding water a kind of signpost.

At Don Sak pier Jamie's body glistened in the afternoon sun. At Phun Phin train station he boarded the old train. He ate pieces of green mango dipped in sugar and chillies and watched children play in the station. Two older boys practiced the latest dance steps. A man carried a boy with no arms or legs through the cars, seeking donations. Finally the train pulled out, night fell and a man came around to prepare the beds.

Samui had been a living dream. Jamie had had the time to dwell on the complexities of a simple orange and the ever changing sky and waters of southern Thailand. For all the colors, the wide spectrums of greens and blues, the mystical purples of twilight reflected on the water, when he would think of Thailand the color would always be gold. A glowing fiery gold, seen at certain sunsets and in the amber of Sunisa's necklace.

A calendar he had picked up at one of the stands provoked a feeling of nostalgia. He remembered the date he had arrived on the island but had shortly thereafter moved into a state of near timelessness. He had seen dates on letters and in the newspapers, of course, but somehow they had held no meaning.

Jamie had been on Samui for three months, but already felt the island changing its hues and fragrances in his memory.

* * * * *

Banglamphu, Bangkok. Jamie settled in a guest house down by the Chao Phraya river.

A notice out front read: No prostitute. No overnight girl. No visiting. No problem making. Violator must be sent to police station and be hold for twenty-four hour investigation.

In reality, farang men and Thai girls came and went as they pleased.

He wandered the city's streets and visited some of the tourist attractions. He took a longtail

Part One

boat to the King's palace where he was confronted with an offering of a pig's head. On a tuk tuk ride back to Khao San Road the driver pointed out the infamous motorcyclists known as the "human flies." Like flies they hung onto their bikes as they raced for high stakes and notoriety. The police could not control them. Jamie thought this driver would have liked to join them in his modified tuk tuk. Bangkok was noisy, dirty, overcrowded and fascinating. Jamie got out by an extensive open market, its stalls filled with a myriad of curiosities. He bought a worn silver ring with the faint impression of a beetle.

Near his guest house was a monastery: besides the saffron robed monks there was a bison, two ponies, cats, dogs and roosters, all co-existing and free from restraint. The monastery was surrounded by ancient walls and had numerous entrances, passageways and courtyards that Jamie explored. In the middle was the glitzy main temple.

At a hotel restaurant Jamie sat down to a disagreeable meal of an overly sweet eggplant stew, so disappointing after the tasty curries and other delicacies of Samui. He spent a few hours nursing drinks. Back at the guest house, sticky from the heat, he took his third shower of the day. The next morning as Jamie passed through the monastery, he was approached by an older man who explained he was Chinese, a guide, a driver, as well as a fortune teller.

"You want to see show? Fuckling? Pussy trick? Ma-sage? How bout clocodile westling? How bout I take you to good tailor vely cheap?" Jamie imagined a suit that fell apart after a week's wear. "How about I tell you what will happen tonight? What you say?"

Jamie didn't say anything. The man smiled.

"How 'bout message from Elias?"

It was Jamie's turn to smile. He was to go to the White Orchid Restaurant in Chinatown. The old man handed him a small wooden box. Inside was a knife. The blade looked as though it had been recently sharpened. An edgy feeling crept over Jamie.

"Real knife not dream knife."

"But what's it for?"

"El Que Vela if he finds you."

At the White Orchid Jamie sat at a small table in the back and watched as people came and went. After having some fish in red sauce and another cocktail he began to fidget. There was nothing happening.

What was he doing here? Was the Committee still after him? Who was El Que Vela?"

Feeling somewhat deranged,

as though lost in the labyrinth of his own mind, Jamie fingered the handle of the knife.

When the restaurant closed he left.

He flagged a cab and near Banglamphu told the cab driver to stop by the entrance of a bar. Brightly painted mermaid statues with idiot eyes flanked the entrance. He went inside. On the ceiling an electric bulb in a rectangular box sputtered and went out. The waiter swept the room with a flashlight until lanterns could be lit. Jamie had another drink before walking back to the guesthouse.

The next morning a blue airmail envelope stamped from India was slid under his door. The note read, "Watch out for El Que Vela, the one who flies. Return to San Francisco. Will be in touch. Elias."

On the plane, eight rows back from Jamie, sat a man in disguise: it was Margo, the Dane. He wore glasses, a brown wig, beard and pretended to be engrossed in a thick paperback. Margo cleared his throat and motioned the stewardess for another drink. Jamie dozed, and in a dream a blackbird appeared. It sat immobile in a velvet lined cage, its eyes glinting in the darkness.

PENNSYLVANIA

Harrisburg. Under a milky sky, gray travelers with red transcendent eyes stood on the banks of the Susquehanna river. In an abandoned house an old science fiction movie was showing on a TV: a man with the face of a lemur wearing a turban was walking through a crystal city. Crowds of apelike people chanted, "The dreamer, the dreamer." Faintly red now the sky held a silver clarity like early morning. Yellow lights, still reflected in the puddles, led the way past an all night diner, a bus station and to the frozen river. The spacecraft sat undisturbed in a thin fog.

The Chief sat in a Committee office reading a report. He lumbered down the hallway and headed for one of the battered elevators. He took it to the basement and walked down an almost identical hall to enter another numbered room.

Inside, patrolman Earl McCray stared at a tin ashtray filled with unfiltered cigarette butts. There was a tape recorder on a wooden table. Against a wall sat a cheaply suited detective and a doctor who wore a white smock and thick glasses. The detective looked bored, the doctor agitated and jumpy.

"Well?" the Chief asked.

Part One

The doctor jerked his chin towards McCray. The Chief took a seat.

"Okey dokey son. It's time to deliver the goods."

Begrudgingly, Earl told his story again. It began when he had identified Elias on Sixth Street entering a storage rental warehouse. McCray was on his way home but had heard a description at a morning briefing; "Hefty, bald, shaved eyebrows and transfixing blue eyes." He pulled over, called in a report, unholstered his revolver and pursued the fugitive into the building.

On the first floor he saw a hooded figure who turned and the room flooded with an overwhelming red light. Three hours later he found himself back in his car.

"But I saw a face!" McCray yelped, wide eyed.

"Well," the Chief said reasonably. "Could you describe it?"

"Yes, in fact I will draw it."

Earl McCray stood at a green chalkboard and erased the remains of some unknown agenda. At first he just stared at the board, then he began to draw a thin human body. He worked with the head until it resembled a kind of owl man. He changed the face to Asian, then Indian, erased that entirely and drew a long bald head with pointed ears, demonic eyes—something like Nosferatu. McCray erased the nose, mouth, ears and changed the eyes to narrow rectangles. The doctor took a Polaroid. The Chief got up and left. McCray suddenly keeled over and died, right then and there, of causes unknown. The coroner's report stated that the heart had simply stopped beating.

* * * * *

El Que Vela, in the dimmest of light, gazed at his wavering reflection in the dark mirror, drifting back to his boyhood. His father was insane and his mother unstable and alcoholic. He had been devoid of emotion the day he was told of their deaths due to a car wreck: just a mildly, pleasant, feeling when he tried to visualize the crash. Soon thereafter he was sent to a "school for troubled boys." He found the discipline feared by the others mild after the treatment he had endured from his parents. He mostly scoffed at the staff's threats and punishments. He was respected by the other boys for his attitude. He relished that respect.

One night he and some others witnessed what was believed to be a ghost in the old dorm. A yellow cloud drifted through the room, seemed to form a human shape, then ascended and disappeared into the "haunted attic." He had been the only one willing to follow it. He told the others that nothing had happened, but he had actually experienced a coolness in his nostrils and a profound surge of energy when he had entered the attic.

Later he felt driven to paint an eye in a box on his wall; he dimmed the lights and stared at the eye. The window slammed shut and locked: the room became airtight and secure as any jail cell. He was thrown back into his chair. The air stirred and his hair stood on end.

He felt the entity had sought him out. Trapped him now. His skin turned white and silky as the air filled with a silvery dust. A hollow eyed man in a dark suit and skull cap stepped out of the shadows and smiled fiendishly. He gestured to the mirror and an owlish thing emerged from it. The man hurried back into the corner.

The entity's eyes were ancient and more hideous than his worst nightmare. The boy felt an unearthly pull: his heart swelled and could have been made to burst, but the thing had let him live. Then it vanished.

"The beloved Enemy," said the man, back from the shadows, in a wavering reverential tone. "You will be El Que Vela."

Over the years El Que Vela had gradually lost his good looks. His dark wavy hair had turned thin and his bedroom eyes had sunk into his head like a Committee man. Deep in the mirror, he bared his jagged teeth and made his arms like short wings, flapping them and laughing hysterically. He stopped when he heard the knock on the door.

The Chief came in hatless. "Why couldn't you have left me in Bangkok?" El Que Vela complained. "Everything was going fine."

"It wasn't going fine. You were starting to bug."

"I was fine. The katoeys were all working for me."

"The katoeys weren't doing shit. I don't understand it," the Chief said. "All of South East Asia. Maybe Vietnam karma."

El Que Vela had been detained after walking naked through the streets of Bangkok in the rain, handing out Committee money. The Chief sat down, crossed a leg, got out his pipe and stuck it into his mouth. He took it out of his mouth and just held it. "Besides," he looked at El Que Vela, who leaned against a wall enjoying the final residue of his annoyance. "We need Elias dead. You're to go to Mexico. Settle in somewhere's. This Jamie Kuhns Coates whatever, will find you and Elias will be there too. The liaison must observe their

Part One

agent's first kill. They must be stopped, goddamn it. They could fuck things up."

* * * * *

When Jamie arrived at SFO he went about the business of getting a cab. The taxi starter waved and one pulled up, manned by an elderly Chinese driver. The driver's thick gray hair was chopped as though cut with hedge shears, just above his frayed collar. Jamie gave him the address. He drove off towards the ticket booth.

The Victorian in Pacific Heights stood before him. Jamie let himself in. The electricity worked. The furniture had not been covered and there was a thick layer of dust over everything. He wandered around and sat in the different rooms. He opened a new letter from Elias that explained that El Que Vela was a Committee agent that could transform into a bird. Elias wrote that he would be contacted by a Mr. Gray. The phone worked and he called Anna. She was excited but on her way to Japan: on assignment.

Jamie practiced the squat, recorded fragments of his dreams and focused on the crimson light which turned a deeper shade and had became a natural part of him. He found the San Francisco weather damp and disagreeable after his stay in the tropics. Restless, he moved around the city and rode the buses, Muni rails and the cable cars. He thought about the stupidity and ugliness of humanity and realized that most of them were not worth saving. The 1 California bus took him to Chinatown. He had breakfast at a restaurant where the cashier stood in a gold cage. The coffee was so strong he drank only one cup and so hot he had to first finish everything else.

A week passed.

Finally he made contact. Mr. Gray was older and had a no-nonsense way about him. He was well read in the esoteric. Mr. Gray had secured a booth in the back of a small restaurant. Jamie got the impression that he had just materialized there. Jamie ordered a sandwich while Mr. Gray had the turkey dinner with all the trimmings. A pretty Chinese waitress swept in the back with quick whisks of her broom.

Mr. Gray said, "I've got your instructions from Elias." Jamie's eyes glinted with interest. "You're going to Mexico. The agent you were to take out in Bangkok is there." Mr. Gray sipped tea and complained out the side of his mouth, it was lukewarm. "A charming little fishing village called San Blás. I was there as a youngster. I was a surfer then. Man, Matanchen Bay, that lovely warm water and that long wave we'd ride all the way to Los Cocos Beach."

Mr. Gray's smile turned flat and serious.

"Have you noticed the empty eyes in this city?"

"Yes. And it's cold."

"The Committee is strong here," Mr. Gray whispered, showing a look of concern. He stirred his tea and looked at it like something was going to happen.

Mr. Gray rubbed his temples. "Elias told you his name is El Que Vela, the one who flies."

"Yes. Elias says he can turn into a bird. Do you believe that?" Mr. Gray didn't answer but ran his thumb across his plate and scooped up gravy, then licked it. Jamie found this vaguely disgusting but didn't say anything. Mr. Gray made a display of licking his front teeth then stared at his plate.

"It's important to spot him before he does you." Mr. Gray said sagely.

The waiter appeared and cleared the table.

* * * * *

Friday night 11:08 P.M. Dressed in an all leather outfit, Margo rode a Kawasaki Eliminator. He had wanted a Harley but couldn't find a place that rented them. Earlier he had gotten out the plastic baggy of methamphetamine. He took his rolled up hundred dollar bill with a little rubber band around it and snorted a line. Now on his "bitch," which was how he referred to the bike, he felt the speed blast through his brain.

Everything was good, he felt. He knew that Jamie Coates was traveling with a passport in the name of "David Kuhns." He knew where he was staying and that he left the house most every morning at around 7 A.M. He knew that usually he caught a bus to Chinatown and ate at the same damn restaurant. El Que Vela had said to tail him and note his movements. He had said, too, that Coates would be offed. So why not just do it? Save them the trouble. That way he could move up in the organization quickly.

Margo figured the next day he would park his bike in Chinatown and position himself in a doorway. As Coates passed by, he would step out and shoot him a couple times in the head using a silencer. Maybe even say something like, "Hey fuckhead, remember me?" or maybe just, "Hey fuckhead": don't want to give him too much play.

He had picked out the spot too, right by where he had seen an old Chinaman selling live frogs

Part One

out of a sack. Coates usually walked that way. El Que Vela had told Margo that a doctor would stop by the hotel for the report and with his pay. He wondered what a fucking doctor had to do with this, he didn't like doctors.

But tonight Margo was celebrating: a little early, but that was his style. He was going to a place where all the lady boys hung out except here they didn't call them lady boys: in fact here they were more like lady men. After his awakening with the katoeys in Bangkok he had discovered that he liked them better than any whore he had ever been with.

Now he was going to a place called the Mother Lode on Post Street. The windows were decorated with glittery purple streamers; inviting only the truly flamboyant to enter. In the windows sat dolled-up trannies from Puerto Rico, Argentina and elsewhere.

Margo had been there two days earlier and after a few beers had started flirting with a transsexual named Christy from Acapulco. "She," was petite, with implanted breasts, expressive eyes and wore a gold cross around her neck. Talking in her ear he had smelled the perspiration partially masked by the French perfume. Back at her room, she had taken his penis into her mouth but he didn't like a look she had given him and he smacked her. She told him to get fucked. Then he got crazy. He left her on the floor of her shabby room, her lip cut badly. She cried out and swore in Spanish that she would hunt him down and slowly kill him.

On the Eliminator, Margo roared down Polk Street and turned on Hemlock Alley. He found a space near Larkin, parked, turned off the engine—and that was the last thing he remembered. Mr. Gray seemed to drop from the sky, grabbing Margo's head by the bottom of his helmet and breaking his neck with the ease of a practiced technician. Mr. Gray dragged the limp body back to a small truck, loaded it in the back and snapped down the cover.

* * * * *

Jamie spent the days eating hardboiled eggs over the sink and playing with Watcher, the black cat who had moved into the house. A package arrived from Pennsylvania: an elegant weapon called a ComBow. It was a combination bow or slingshot, depending on the band. Jamie thought it looked like something out of an apocalyptic science fiction story.

He read that this precision weapon, made from metal used in aircraft construction, was used for deer hunting. It had a molded hand grip and a piece of metal that fitted snugly on his forearm. On either side tubes held the surgical rubber band. The short arrows were called bolts.

Jamie made a target out of a box stuffed with newspapers. He played a tape, "Sounds of the Everglades," while he practiced. San Blás sounded a lot like the Everglades, from what he had read. He found the weapon to his liking. Jamie put himself into different moods and different lighting and practiced.

He stared into the mirror. He made a circle and watched a red light replica of himself emerge from the mirror.

A few days later a blue airmail envelope arrived, posted from Washington D. C. A one-way ticket on Mexicana Airlines to Puerto Vallarta. Then Jamie received a call from Mr. Gray who told him about Margo. He offered some more suggestions about San Blás and El Que Vela. He would come by in the morning to pick up Watcher.

Jamie drew a bird on the target box.

MEXICO

The cab dropped Jamie at the Pacifico bus station. His timing was good. Fifteen minutes later he was settling into a well worn seat as the old bus pulled out of town. Mounted on the dash was a gold Jesus-on-the-cross, adorned with blue-and-red plastic flowers and surrounded by a red velour frame. The driver was playing traditional Mexican music updated with electric guitar and what sounded like a Moog. The passengers were all Mexican: men in sombreros and girls with beat up luggage. Children hawked junk food at stops, passengers got off, others got on. The bus traveled through a mountainous area past dusty villages and jungles of twisted trees. The smell of burning leaves came from the roadside cemeteries erected in memory of accident victims. Children played by huge open structures where tobacco dried. Jamie watched the setting sun in the evening sky unroll a swirl of Technicolor, the rising pollution only adding to the varied richness of its hues and whorls.

The old bus sped down the unknown roads and twice passed slow moving trucks blind. It pulled into town under a full moon. It was late and only a few faceless men were on the streets.

At a hotel on Juarez a deep emptiness settled over Jamie as he sat in the gloomy room. In the morning the clop clopping of

Part One

hooves on the cobblestone stirred him from sleep. A water wagon crawled by, pulled by two horses, its driver monotonously clanging on an old bell. Jamie looked at a map. The town of San Blás was on the Pacific coast about midway between Mazatlan and Puerto Vallarta.

In the courtyard there was a coati chained to a tree. It had a long snout, ringed tail, claws and seemed quite intelligent to Jamie. Locally it was known as a tajon. "The coati is from the raccoon family," he would read later at the local library. Jamie stopped and petted it. It was tame but still possessed a manic quality and Jamie left before it became overexcited.

By the afternoon Jamie was sitting on an overturned boat at the port, watching an old trawler being pumped. He began to feel stings on his arms and watched the red welts appear: it was the "no see 'ums" he had read about. He applied some lotion. A few pelicans and smaller birds stood immobile on the muddy shore. The smell of algae mixed with the dust and the heat. Above a tall clump of large leafed plants, frigate, grackle and other birds he didn't recognize flew about. An iguana emerged from some rocks and hurried away.

Following the inlet from the port, Jamie came across a group of fishermen and their boats. He tried out some of the Spanish he was learning from a phrase book with one of them. The fishermen had cleaned their catch and the purple squared off raw fish sat in neat stacks on the cement. Some of the men just sat and looked at them. The others smoked and talked quietly amongst themselves. An iguana moved awkwardly across some rocks.

Jamie walked a dirt road past adobe houses and came to a long strip of tarmac with a tire on its side at each end. In a booth sat a blue uniformed guard bored with the minor airfield. A truck with a Fender amp strapped on its roof rolled by, the driver announcing something in Spanish.

He crossed the road to a juice bar. Jamie considered a banana, papaya and pineapple drink made by a fat Mexican with a Hitler mustache. A wall poster advertised an upcoming "transvestites" show. Jamie wondered if the truck driver had been announcing the same show.

The fat Mexican poured the thick juice into two glasses, stuck a straw in one. He pulverized carrots for two Mexicans with his high-powered juicer.

A big box of batteries behind the counter reminded Jamie of a story an old cab driver had told him. The man had been driving

PORTS OF HELL

through remote country somewhere in the Sierra Madres and had come across a group of Indians with a burro and cart full of batteries. They had come from a PeMex station, a trip they made from their village twice a year to recharge the old batteries.

On the walk back Jamie came across Mexican women cooking fish on wide black grills by the river. He climbed a cobblestone road past a cemetery and the ruins of an olden cathedral. He reached the remains of an equally old fort at the top of the hill. A couple of iguana disappeared into the crumbling foundations.

The sea spread out before him. There was a red-and-white striped lighthouse on a small island, some other villages and wandering waterways that connected with either of the two border estuaries. Wide golden fields made their way to tall slate colored mountains that resembled reclining Gods of the Mayans and Aztecs. Around him stood old black cannons and he thought of the day's long ago, when galleon from the Far East had come to this port and there had been pirate attacks and cannon fire.

Overhead a vulture flew by.

Back down on the road he watched an old man peddle by. There were lots of bicycles in the town, many with funny wheel combinations. Most had extended axles to accommodate a second standing rider. Everyone rode slowly, there being no reason to hurry. Two men in white naval uniforms peddled by, a common sight since the Mexican navy had a base there.

Jamie had dinner with an old timer who wore a baseball cap with "100% Loco" emblazoned on the front. Jamie had said he liked it. "I'm loco but not stupid," was the reply. Jamie had a hunch he was a contact.

The old timer had been living in San Blás for nine years, a permanent resident at the hotel where Jamie was staying. His glasses hung from his neck by a piece of string. He spoke fondly about a boat he had owned that had been equipped with all the latest technology. He claimed that people lost in jungles and other remote areas could survive if they just had a Boy Scout field manual. He proudly named all the guns he had owned and gave special praise to a "riot gun". "I took on five men in Durango with it," he said smiling proudly. The old timer ate his lunch of fried fish, tortillas and beans.

"I don't eat no fruits or vegetables," he explained. Jamie asked him if he took any vitamins and he said sometimes.

Jamie mentioned the beautiful

Part One

and plentiful women of Thailand to see if that interested him. The old timer wanted to know if what he had heard about AIDS there was a scare job by the government. Jamie said that Eric who lived there believed just that. Eric felt it was engineered by the religious right and the radical feminists. "Strange bedfellows," the old timer commented. "But I believe it."

The old timer scratched his chin, became thoughtful, "I'm gonna go there. I got a plastic dick." He grinned. "It goes up and it don't come down." Jamie could easily see him there with old Pete and the others.

The old timer jumped around from topic to topic; dogs with rabies, coyotes, scorpions and fire ants, which he said will go out of their way to sting a man. "I've seen 'em all over a man before he knows it." He dabbed his face with a paper napkin. He drew a circle on the table.

"Now on the subject of birds," he bared his broken yellow teeth. "You've got your hands full with El Que Vela. Have you taken a look at the old mission? That place is a hot spot."

The old timer put his glasses back on. They paid their bills, each leaving a five peso tip. Out on the street, the old timer let out a loud fart.

At the empty soccer stadium Jamie climbed the steps of the spectator stands. Behind was the ocean and the sound of the surf. The soccer field gave way to another field, some brush and then jungle. Above that, on a prominent hill, was the old mission. Over the years the place had faded, peeled and mildewed.

Jamie felt a haunted and hostile essence emanated from it. Birds flew overhead, squawked and whistled in a depraved way. He could just barely see a weak light coming from inside, a faint but weird greenish glow.

Three locals appeared from the beach with their dogs. Jamie was startled for a moment but they moved on, heading across the field. One carried an inner tube on his back and another wore a white seaman's cap. The oldest had a bushy gray mustache and a machete sheathed in a copper colored leather. The dogs ran ahead and disappeared into the jungle. Jamie decided they were oyster fishermen. Earlier, on the beach, he had came across a plump blue rat washed onto the shore. And a large gutted fish, an army of flies feasting in its open belly.

Jamie's shadow projected over the stadium seats and made him appear thirty feet tall. The blue shadow of the mountain range was falling across the land. A plastic cup on the bottom row was arcing back and forth in the wind. Jamie crouched, trying to somehow read the sky, the mountains or the birds. He pressed his amulet between his fingers.

A gang of local boys were stopped at a fence. One climbed over, jumped down and grabbed the tail of an iguana that stuck out of a deep crevice between two boulders. He laughed moronically as his pals looked on. He tried to lift the creature out but it was firmly dug in. Without letting go, the boy found a stick and stuck it in the crevice banging it about, trying to get the iguana to give up its grip—still it would not budge.

The boy pulled hard with both hands and the tail snapped off. He yelled and threw it to the ground where it writhed back and forth. His friends laughed uneasily. Jamie standing with a small crowd felt a wave of disgust. An insect flew into his mouth. He thought he spat it out.

When the boy climbed back over the fence a man in a suit grabbed him by the shirt and drew a finger across his throat. The boy shook free and pantomimed a tail growing back. Then he ran off laughing with his friends. Jamie had the sensation that something harmful had lodged in the core of his stomach. Back at the hotel he told the old timer about the iguana.

"Yeah, a tail will grow back in time," the old timer said. "That tail moving on its own is a defense mechanism. An enemy that has bit it off will think it's another creature." He glanced around. "You have enemies too, Jamie. Keep your wits about you."

Jamie told him about the stomach pain.

"I think it's time ya visited Tony the Indian, also known as Indian Tony, also known as just Tony."

* * * * *

Back at the mission El Que Vela poured himself another cup of mescal. He threw it down and bared his teeth. He poured himself another and threw that down. His expression settled gradually to a look of bemused calmness. It was a good exercise to measure the other agent's sensory capabilities he decided. Now he would see if Jamie Coates was a worthy adversary. If he could expel the bug he would rethink and replot the course that would unfold between them.

* * * * *

"Hi man, what's up?" Indian Tony asked Jamie who stood in the doorway.

Part One

Tony the Indian gestured Jamie to a seat. White room. Bare except for a white wooden table and two white plastic chairs. Out the window, countless cumulus clouds in the Mexican sky. Tony's eyes were smoky gray. He was dressed in black and had straight, black, shoulder length hair. He wore a collection of silver bracelets and an opal talisman of the sun.

Jamie told him the story.

Tony rolled a joint and shook his head. "El Que Vela," he said thickly. "He pulled a stall on you man. You know that, right?" He lit up, took a few puffs and passed it.

"He put a bug in you man. Where's the pain?"

Tony poked at the spot Jamie pointed out. Jamie flinched as he felt something begin to move there in his stomach.

"What kind of bug?"

"Yellow bug. Enemy. Committee insect."

Tony placed his palm there and told Jamie to breath slowly and push out his diaphragm. Tony chanted under his breath. Jamie felt it move through his chest cavity, up his throat and with a buzz out of his mouth. It left behind a sour taste. Jamie made a face and Tony handed him a cup of tea.

"Drink."

Fighting nausea, Jamie gulped down the bitter brew. The sickness passed and the taste in his mouth turned to that of mint. Jamie had seen nothing, but Tony stood looking out the window as if to catch a glimpse. Jamie looked too but saw only the dusty Mexican landscape.

"Bug agent will die now," Tony said.

Tony told him he was a Huichol shaman like his father had been. His mother was a Cora—Coras were mostly farmers. Jamie pressed him about the Huichols. Tony's grandfather had told him that the tribe had come from a lost world in Asia. He said they had crossed the Bering Straits on long boats and had migrated southward. They were originally warriors, but after discovering peyote they had converted to shamanism and artistry.

He showed Jamie a book filled with their magical drawings of animals, flowers and the cosmos of inner space. Tony offered him a small seed cake wrapped in paper. It tasted of cinnamon, honey and an exotic mix of nuts and seeds.

At the port, a heavy set man and a slightly effeminate man stood talking. Jamie had followed them from the old mission. Fats wore a sombrero and the other a baseball cap. They walked off in separate directions. Jamie decided to follow the sombrero. After ten minutes, Fats went through a blue wooden door into a narrow house with no front windows. Jamie marked the location on a small hand drawn map. He headed back the cobblestone alleys past the high fences made of long crooked sticks, past the boys who practiced the lariat, girls their ballerina steps, women cooking on grills, roosters pecking, cats sleeping and a donkey, it's cart empty, standing by the side of the road.

Sunset at the zócalo. Jamie held something that looked like a bomb. It was actually an orange drink that's container was black and round. It had a tall neck with a red stopper. Jamie sat on a white wrought iron bench and drank some of the juice then blew into the plastic container to restore its round shape. In a gazebo a group of kids played at some mysterious game. There was a stone fountain over at one end and a stage was being erected for an upcoming fiesta. Jamie wondered if anyone had ever been hung in the square.

On one of the churches nearby a plaque was inscribed with a fragment by Longfellow from The Bells of San Blás, in which he found the bells to create "a strange wild melody." Having listened to the incredible bird sounds Jamie wondered why he hadn't mentioned them instead— he found them much stranger than the church bells. The sounds they achieved in San Blás seemed to affect people and everywhere there was whistling, wild laughter and unusual music. The old timer said that Longfellow had never even been to San Blás but had written that poem up at Mazatlán. "Because if he had,' the old timer winked, "he would have called it The Bugs of San Blás."

Jamie walked by piles of oyster shells on broken sidewalks that led to rubble then sand. He caught the slightly sickly smell of overripe bananas, mangos and papaya. He overheard some gringos talking about their jungle boat trip and how thrilled they were when a crocodile had headed in their direction. They had passed through mangrove lowlands by lagoons where wild puma still lived. Long hikes would soon be taken outside of the town, but first Jamie would began the morning regimen he had developed on the island. He remembered how sharp he had felt on the beaches of Koh Samui. He sensed the seaside already beginning to rejuvenate him.

From his porch Jamie could see a section of the El Pozo estuary which led inward towards the port. Humming a marimba tune he made his way down to the

Part One

beach. By one of the palapa-styled restaurants the effeminate man sat by himself on a small rectangle of a towel drinking a coke. His blue Florida baseball cap shaded his eyes. The man finished off the Coke and tossed the empty bottle to the ground. On the other side of the incline Jamie found a cove where some rocks jutted out of the blue black sea. Three Mexican boys were there. They said hi and waded into the water.

Jamie climbed down and cut across the beach and entered some tall weeds to urinate. The effeminate man was there in front of him, aiming a pistol with a steady look in his violet shaded eyes. His eyebrows were drawn in like a San Blás prostitute.

"Give up your money gringo!"

Jamie complied and handed over a wad of peso notes. He was actually calm.

"Your wallet!" he demanded gesturing for Jamie to throw it at his feet as he took a few steps back. Jamie figured he would grab it and run off. But a perverse smile came across the man's lips and he gestured with the gun.

"Now your clothes."

Jamie had a strong hunch he would not shoot. He began obediently to take off a shoe; then faked a stumble and grabbed hold of the gun. He slammed it to the side of the man's face who cried out and slumped from the impact. Jamie took back the money and his wallet.

"I want you and your friend to vamoose San Blás."

He looked at Jamie askance. His nose trickled blood.

"And where's El Que Vela?" Jamie demanded.

The young man got to his feet. He crossed himself. "I'm finished with his—" He searched for a word unsuccessfully. "He ez at the mission," he said solemnly and motioned in that direction. "*Si*, I leave *sénor*." The young man wiped the blood from his nose and felt an ear, thankful the gold ring was still intact. Jamie told him to get on his way and he did.

Jamie urinated and walked back to the beach. He sidestepped a crab as he walked into the white foamy green ocean. A liquid white sun was reflected in its waves. He heard the pop sound of gunfire in the distance. He fingered the gun in his back pocket.

When Jamie got out of the water two German shepherds came towards him down the empty beach. They flanked him and laid down. Their eyes were savage and they showed their teeth. Jamie passed by; they growled then whimpered but they did not move.

On the road a family of Huichol Indians adorned in their brightly colored clothes passed by. Some boys peddled newspapers. Nobody seemed interested. A pickup truck rolled by. In the bed of the truck, Mexicans slouched in lawn chairs. Jamie looked at his map and headed down a sandy street where previous foot prints were being erased by the wind. Twenty minutes later he came to the house with the blue wooden doors.

In the shadows of an entranceway of an abandoned building Jamie swirled a serape around himself. He closed his eyes. Time seemed to slow as the red glow pulsed and the trance state came over him. The doors at the house opened and a pretty girl appeared and threw out a bucket of water. When she turned to get her broom to continue her ritual of sweeping the dirt into the air, Jamie entered like a phantom. He found the bedroom and pulled out the gun. There was the sleeping body. This was the portly man, nice pleasant face, mustache that extended a bit past his lip. Jamie hovered above him. He banged his chin with the butt handle. The man groaned, opened his eyes and stayed still as though paralyzed.

"*Habla Ingles*?"

"*Si*. Yes, *sénor*," he said with wide eyes.

"Where is El Que Vela?"

A funny gurgling noise came from his throat, then he whispered:

"The old mission."

"Where?"

"Above the stadium. He and our dogs." Jamie showed him a different angle of the barrel. The man licked his lips and smiled weakly. "I leave with my son. We go to Guadalajara. The dogs will come too if I whistle from the stadium."

Jamie moved backwards. He danced past the woman still sweeping and two little girls on bikes at the entrance of an iron gate who called out "Nina, Nina," in unison, but Nina didn't appear to be home.

Had he scared off El Que Vela's boys? He hoped so. He lunched at a little place where the walls were decorated with sea shells, fishing nets and nautical what-have-yous. The smell, too, was of the sea, odorous yet tolerable, like a well-meaning but drunk sailor. A child waitress with a green-yellow parakeet on her shoulder took his order.

He tipped back the bowl to spoon up the remaining soup when a fly nose-dived into his coffee and died there. Jamie scooped it out with a spoon and placed it on the saucer. He looked at it for a minute, picked it up with his fingers and dropped it onto the floor. It was too hot and he was too tired to think much about it. Jamie stirred the coffee

Part One

and took a sip. Through the open door he saw the father and son. He moved further out of sight. They got into an old green Buick, the German shepherds in the back. In the open door's glass Jamie watched the reflection of the car as it headed out of town.

* * * * *

El Que Vela had been up late drinking and talking to himself. He had cursed the father and son for being so chicken shit. He would take care of this intruder. Put his head on a stick. That always impressed them. Then he would feed them the agent's heart to bolster their meager human stamina. His mouth was dry and he wished he had stopped for a beer, but first he had to get an important call out of the way. He walked across the square and went into the old bus station where he made all his long distance calls. He took a booth and dialed.

"Chief?"

"Yes. Report."

"The kid's here. He's chased off the father and son."

"Elias?"

"No, no. Nothing yet. Just the new agent. Spooked my team. I'm gonna fuck him up."

"Not yet. Turn into a bird until the time's right. Until Elias."

"Yeah. Okay."

"I repeat we must have Elias is the same vicinity. Go to Mexico City. He'll follow."

* * * * *

A darkly tanned man in need of a shave and a diet was sitting near Jamie's porch. A briefcase sat next to him. He wore a fishing hat and a white T-shirt that had been round necked but was re-cut into a V. A small rectangular contraption was connected to his hat band and another at the top of knee-high socks. Jamie could hear a high frequency sound.

"That there's the Expeller," the man said and introduced himself as Calver in an overly friendly manner. "It expels mosquitoes and other biting insects," he said. "San Blás is lousy with em and jenenes, known as no see 'ums."

Having bought a heavy-duty repellent that the military used in the jungles of Central America (so the container claimed), Jamie was well aware of all that, but he was still getting bit. Calver explained that the only mosquito that bit was the pregnant female and that the Expeller imitated the sonic sound of the male mosquito and kept the pregnant females away.

"Now nothing is a hundred

percent," he said with a cagey look. "But ya know this is the mosquito capital and I've walked all over an only been bit twice. And I don't have the Expeller on all the time."

He patted the case beside him. Half believing the sales pitch and deciding it would be a curio, if nothing else, Jamie bought one. Besides, he was sick of applying the vaguely foul repellent twice daily, and willing to try a new method. Jamie clipped it to his waist.

Calver brought out a bottle of Ronrico rum and they moved to a table by the pool. One of the hotel girls arrived, as if on cue, with glasses, ice, lime and Coca Cola. Calver fished a plastic container out of his briefcase.

"Chapala cheese. Something for us to munch on. Don't 'cha worry, I've kept it refrigerated."

Calver laughed and said if Jamie got bit now the mosquito was either deaf or gay. They sipped the drinks and listened to the high frequency sounds of the Expeller's mixing with the night sounds of the insects. A blonde lady walked by on the other side of the pool. Calver called out:

"Hey d' ya know why blondes have more fun?"

She stopped and turned for a minute. "No, do tell," she said but resumed walking.

"Because ya can see 'em in the dark," he called out. Calver laughed into his drink. "There's two things I've found that follow no particular logic. Know what they are? Mexico and women, no logic what—so—ever."

Calver polished off his drink and made another.

"Is there a place in town where the ladies show off their girlies?" he asked with a lewd wink.

Jamie told him the names of the dance halls where the whores, for a price, would certainly oblige him.

Jamie wondered if the *señorita* who had ignited his imagination earlier that day was there dancing under the flickering lights. She had been standing in a doorway, her face overly made up yet compelling. She had turned slowly to show him her backside.

Calver freshened Jamie's drink and unrolled a newspaper. He donned a pair of glasses that sat on the end of his nose and began to read.

"January 23rd, Mineral Wells, Texas. Three men were electrocuted while trying to steal copper wire from an electrical system. The metal is valuable as scrap." He sat the paper down.

"Well, doesn't appear I've missed too much."

What about Calver? Jamie couldn't check with the old timer since he had gone to Mexico City. They walked into town and took

Part One

a table at the most popular spot on the zócalo. They ate and heard the chatter of the birds which roosted in the big trees. These birds sang, chirped and yakked for their spots every night. Not a lot different from the dozen or so ex-pats, who gathered nightly and laid claim to certain tables. Leaning against a wall some women knitted and talked. Ex-drunkards sipped mineral waters and tried to outdo each other with sour expressions.

Eventually the talk got around to the bugs. Was it the mosquitoes or the "no see 'ums?" The repellent currently being touted, Avon's Face So Soft, was not intended as such but it was supposed to work. Before long Calver had a small crowd at the table. Most were skeptical but he managed a few sales. So far the thing seemed to be working for Jamie.

A young Mexican boy appeared, struggling to seem at least as tall as the table. Instead of trying to sell the usual stale packets of Chicolets, this young entrepreneur offered something in a baggy: a half dead mouse. The tiny thing tried to crawl to the top but was slowly being asphyxiated. Calver waved the kid away. A woman bought the mouse at the exorbitant price of thirty pesos and, with much ado, took it out to the street and released it to an unknown fate.

Jamie watched the birds and wondered if El Que Vela was amongst them. As he got up to leave Calver called out that he would be by in the morning.

At the top of a hill, Jamie dropped to the squatting position and focused his camera zoom on the old mission. There was no sign of life. He scanned the dusty streaked windows, some broken. He took a photograph.

Suddenly it was as though he was three times stronger and sharper. A red light of his image emerged from the camera and glided across the landscape. Through the zoom he watched it go through a wall.

He was there. Everything was in black and white, and slightly jerky like a damaged film. A befouled mattress lay in a corner. A trail of feathers led across the room to a pile of dirty laundry. Dishes crowded the sink. Water dripped from the tap. El Que Vela was gone. The reconnaissance completed, Jamie directed himself back and the camera was still pressed to his face. He tasted metal. Mosquitoes swarmed all around him. He had forgotten the Expeller; he batted at them and hurried down the hill. At the bottom a gang of watery eyed children not unlike the mosquitoes swarmed around him. Jamie handed out coins to the greedy hands that tapped at his pockets.

PORTS OF HELL

Leaning in a doorway Indian Tony called out. "*Hola amigo. Mio como estás?*"

"*Hola* my friend. *Másomenos.*" Jamie told him about a dull pain in his shin. He didn't know where it had come from. Tony squatted and felt the spot.

"If it gets worse use ice. *El está tratando de lastimarte.* He tries to cripple you in dead dreams."

When Jamie told Tony that El Que Vela had disappeared from the mission, Tony nodded but looked suspiciously at some birds that flew high overhead.

* * * * *

Calver sat by the pool. Judging by the ashtray he was smoking his third cigarette. Calver said: "What did Jesus say at the last supper?"

Jamie shrugged.

"Give Judas the check, he got paid today." Calver laughed loudly.

"Okay what did Jesus say at the last supper?" he persisted.

Jamie shrugged again.

"Separate checks." Calver laughed some more, thoroughly enjoying the joke the more he told it.

"Hey, d'ya know they're making Mercedes Benz now in Mexico? They're called Mercedes Beans." He laughed just softly at this, embarrassed over enjoying himself so much.

Disconnected and uneasy, having lost El Que Vela, Jamie excused himself, went into his room and poured a glass of water from the pitcher on the dresser. Back outside, he sat down. Calver flipped ash off his cigarette. A young girl rode by on her bicycle. Calver followed her with a depraved stare and murmured:

"Oh honey, where d'you park your bike so I can sniff the seat."

Jamie bristled.

"You know about Semana Santa?" Calver drawled in his good nature-I'll-bore-you-to-death manner. "From Palm Sunday to Easter Sunday ya don't wanna be anywhere near any beaches. Mexicans, Mexicans and more Mexicans. Their garbage and dirty diapers are everywhere. The streets are all jammed up and everyone's blastin' their goddamn horns and the gas fumes are chokin' you to death."

"That's nearly two weeks away," Jamie said, still irked.

Calver changed the subject and with a display of concern asked how the Expeller was working. Jamie alluded to some bites but admitted to having forgotten it. He left Calver on the porch and went in to take a shower. As he was getting undressed, he overheard him talking to some new arrivals.

"Friends, d'ya know this is the

Part One

mosquito capitol?"

Someone knocked at Jamie's door and said that he had a telephone call.

"Hello Elias?"

"El Que Vela is gone man gone."

"Yes, I'll find him."

"No problem—but where, Jamie boy?"

"See somebody named Pepe," Jamie said. The words coming into his head as the line went dead.

At twilight in the zócalo Jamie shelled peanuts and watched a local with sombrero tilted and a droopy mustache trot his pale horse down the cobblestone street. He asked around but no one knew a Pepe. He was on guard and half expected El Que Vela to appear and force him into a showdown. And he still wondered about Calver; he spotted him in the doorway of a cantina. He peered at Jamie over a newspaper.

"Hey Jamie. Listen to this," he called out. "Roubaix, France. The cadaver of a local man was discovered sitting on his sofa in front of a still-lit television about ten months—"

A loud motor drowned him out. A sprayer on the back of an approaching truck bombarded the landscape with clouds of poison. People hurried away, covered their mouths with their hands or with their shirts. Later Jamie heard that the sprayers were sent out because the governor and some other big cheese were coming to town for a few hours. And he learned from the old timer that Calver too was a contact.

Calver had checked out. Jamie looked at the Expeller as though seeing it for the first time. Calver's cover had been as an obnoxious, traveling salesman. Jamie listened and tried to connect to the Expeller's frequency. It led him into the courtyard of the hotel where he had first stayed. The coati was still there and appeared excited at seeing him. The animal rolled over on its back offering its stomach for a rub. A maid leaned on her broom, looked out from a doorway. The animal righted itself, twittered, sniffed the air with its long snout and seemed to point to a skinny Mexican man who was sprawled on a bench. He wore rubber sandals, shorts no longer than underpants and a Raiders tank top. He was asleep.

The maid said, *"Pepe el boracho."* She shook her head. "No *bueno* that one. Just out of pre-zone."

When the maid went back to her work, Jamie rustled Pepe awake. The man reeked of alcohol but kept his eyes open and smiled rat-like through broken teeth. Jamie pressed him against his protests, demanding to know where El Que Vela was. The Mexican motioned across the courtyard to an open door.

Inside, the room held the gloomy smell of confinement that he still carried with him. His eyes glistened in the near dark and in a throaty whisper said:

"Go to PV, man. Puerto Vallarta. El Que Vela is waiting..."

In front of the hotel the old timer and Jamie sat on a worn wooden bench in the shade. A hunchback walked by and they said buenos tardes. The old timer said that the hunchback worked at another hotel. They said buenos tardes again when a partially paralyzed woman limped by. The old timer said she too worked at the same hotel. He asked Jamie for the gun and said he must use his own weapons.

Jamie stood before the two churches across from the square. One was so old it served as a museum. Inside that one Jamie discovered a smell that made him think of a Tibetan monastery. Dimly lit pictures of its history lined a wall. Off to one side a choir of children were being led by a dwarf on an antique organ. The choir was having difficulty getting the timing right. The dwarf stopped and made them count and clap between verses.

In the second church Jamie took a pew. He looked around at the replicas of saints at the altar. He dropped a ten peso coin into an old collection box at the feet of some saint and mumbled some half remembered Latin. The box sounded empty. There were more boxes by other saints and Jamie began to put one in each, but found he only had twenty peso coins so he left instead.

As Jamie ate breakfast he watched the street being doused with buckets of water. A red wall's reflection in the early light made the street appear red as well. At one table sat a dusty group of old ex-pats. One with a wooden leg leaned on a crutch and spoke to another about AA.

"Now ya gotta be sincere," he said. "And if ya wanna sponsor I'll help ya out there."

The guy didn't look like he wanted a sponsor and didn't say anything. Another old prospector changed the subject saying he had just gotten the new Soldier of Fortune magazine. Decked out in the latest backpacker gear Dr. Hunter and his female companion walked along Juarez. Somehow Jamie wasn't surprised. They went into the courtyard of the Flamingo Hotel. Jamie finished his breakfast and walked over to the Flamingo. In the courtyard, Hunter sat in the shade hunched over a laptop. His

Part One

lady companion wore extravagant winged sunglasses and sipped a tall drink from a straw. Jamie crossed the square to the bus station to inquire about a ticket. Approaching the station he spotted the three Committee agents getting out of a taxi. Jamie stepped behind a tree. They wore black suits, berets and had sunken eyes. They each carried an identical small piece of luggage and walked off in the same direction.

* * * * * *

"Go to PV man. El Que Vela is waiting."

After checking into a hotel in Puerto Vallarta Jamie took a walk around town. The foliage was all neatly trimmed and everything looked freshly painted for the teams of tourists who frequented the hotels and hives of shops and restaurants. Jamie found a sparsely populated spot on the beach and sunbathed. Some Mexican kids in the water tossed an orange into the air, seeing who could retrieve it amongst the crashing waves. A man sharpened sticks for the hordes of boys who hawked the small fish and would cook it on the spot. Someone wolf-whistled and an American beauty turned around, whereas the aloof Mexican ladies would not. A boy came by and handed Jamie a coupon announcing a hot legs contest. He looked for a sign, a clue and began to scrutinize a too friendly waiter, a hawker, a policeman in his white jungle outfit, pith helmet and Bermuda shorts who seemed to turn up everywhere.

The next evening, as Jamie was passing through a maze of gardens, souvenir shops and ice cream parlors he got the notion he was being shadowed. A hood hid the stalker's face. He was dressed in gray, a small bag slung over a shoulder. Jamie had a strong hunch it was El Que Vela. He hurried down an alley, stepped into a dark doorway and got out his knife. Nothing happened.

Back at the hotel he saw the door ajar. He had waited too long.

Jamie loaded the ComBow and pulled a bolt back taut. Inside, his gear was strewn about. A favorite shirt was ripped down the middle. El Que Vela had urinated somewhere. There were a few bird feathers on the floor. A trace of manic psychic energy remained in the room. The Expeller sat on a newspaper on top of the desk, its high frequency sound speaking to him.

"Step into Mexico City." a pleasing yet inhuman voice whispered in his ear.

"Step into Mexico City."

Jamie stared at a framed black

and white photograph of Mexico City. It came to life expanding and covering the entire wall. Jamie picked up the Expeller and stepped into it.

El Que Vela stood in a dusty phone booth and listened to the phone ringing a thousand miles away. His purplish lips moved about nervously. Across the street a woman threw out a bucket of brackish water from a plastic pail. A group of street urchins ran by. One, his face painted white, stuck out his tongue. El Que Vela found the traffic, noise and people stimulating after the too quiet period at the old mission. Finally the Chief picked up the line.

"It's me."

"Where the fuck are you? What happened?"

"Mexico City. I need a place though."

"Elias?"

"You want him bad, eh?"

"Yes, are you okay?"

"Yeah."

El Que Vela saw the white faced kid heading towards a weedy vacant lot. He overtook him and wrestled him behind a gutted Volkswagen and quickly slit his throat. Mesmerized with the dead white face, he smeared the blood in circles around the boy's eyes until he was aroused. He lurched away, down an empty subway staircase, wildly stabbing a woman, who shrieked before falling as she grasped at her wounds.

Wasting no time he got to the bottom and boarded a train. As always after violence his blood felt cool. He had ejaculated in his pants. He wanted more but decided to find the address the Chief had given him.

A taxi let him off in front of a crumbling colonial home. He climbed the steps and entered a dusty room. He stood in front of a full-length oval mirror. He raised his arms and flapped them like wings.

"Disconnect," he commanded his reflection and voices and images drifted back and through him.

The Committee had selected him to be the bird. At first an ugly, gawkish, land clinging, feathered thing that's voice sounded not unlike a muffled scream. Then, thanks to the Japanese techie, the first good transformation had taken place.

Next he set up Operation Katoey. His original man in Thailand, the old German, had been assassinated. Found in a bungalow on Koh Samui. The old shit had been an inside man and had gotten him through all the paperwork to run a couple of bars that the katoeys could work. But then Jamie Coates had shown up and everything was fucked.

Then he saw how he could use

Part One

the new guy, Margo. Give him some time to relocate, since that was what the Committee wanted. At the mission he had received news of Margo's disappearance. He had cursed and caused such havoc that the men and dogs had left the premises. That was the night he had taken Rosita, a local whore, down to the empty beach and jammed the rail spike up her. The next day the police arrested the local idiot who had been seeing her and sent him off to prison in Tepic. El Que Vela laughed remembering all this. In the mirror his face remained sinister, hawk like, and his eyes glinted in the darkness that had settled in the room.

At an old monastery, converted into a hotel (a Howard Johnson, no less), Jamie knocked for five minutes before someone let him in. He slept poorly and began to dread a confrontation with El Que Vela, which seemed like a confrontation with himself.

At daybreak he boarded the subway, then a bus. Jamie followed the sound of the Expeller and the pulse of his inner red light. On the city's outskirts he walked a boulevard and through a decorative plaza made his way up a plateau where decaying colonial homes lined the crest of a cliff. At the last one he stopped. The Expeller had begun to screech and the light in his head was like a glowing red globe. Jamie turned it off. The door was open. He stepped into the foyer and crept up a dimly lit staircase.

With the ComBow loaded he moved into an open room. Jamie sensed another presence and fired at a moving blur. The bolt stuck in the wall and quivered there. El Que Vela stepped out from behind an overstuffed bookcase and took a bow, gracefully, silently. His mouth held a strange leer and Jamie paused. A look of sadness was in his eyes and his thin, yellowish face seemed to drop. Then his mouth opened and exposed jagged and splintered teeth. His face was now a spasm of anger. "Are you ready for your death?" He screeched in a piercing voice and glared at Jamie hatefully, insanely.

He jerked his head back and forth. A chill spread over Jamie. At that moment El Que Vela pulled a short sword and rushed him. Jamie got to the wall and twisted wildly to escape his thrust.

Jamie hammered the side of his head with the ComBow, since he had lost his second bolt. Stunned, El Que Vela dropped, then retrieved the sword but moved away. Jamie fired another bolt deep into his side. El Que Vela shrieked, dropped the sword again and staggered away. El Que Vela broke off the bolt and ex-

PORTS OF HELL

tended his arms like Jesus on the cross, his yellow eyes blazing. Then there was a flash of light that blinded Jamie and El Que Vela transformed into a large, fluttering, pearl colored bird with flinty yellow eyes.

But there were two other birds as well; all were identical. The birds screeched and flew about the room. Jamie let something inside take over and fired another bolt. Another flash like the first. He shielded his eyes. The birds disappeared and El Que Vela, with the bolt in his heart, stumbled out to the balcony and collapsed.

From the ledge of the balcony Jamie looked out at the stained skyline. Somehow his forearm had been slashed. Like a new Tezcatlipoca, the sorcerer Aztec god who initiated human sacrifice, known as the Warrior, the Smoking Mirror, the Nocturnal Wind, Tez for short, Jamie cupped the bright blood and splashed it through the thick air toward the sun.

By the wall, Jamie took off his T-shirt and wrapped his arm. There he sat for an hour, in silence. A surge had come into his heart and everything seemed to have been happening at some other place simultaneously. And he felt someone had been watching and listening, too.

Voices and movement came from inside the house. Jamie loaded the ComBow, turned and fired a direct hit through a Committee agent's neck. The Committee man grabbed at the bolt, sputtered, walked into a wall and fell down. A pool of blood began to form like a big red beard. Jamie was ready with another bolt but then Elias stepped out onto the balcony with his hand raised as if to begin waving goodbye to the dead men. Elias had shaved his mustache and eyebrows and was wearing his hooded robe. Inside, two other Committee agents were hung from ceiling beams on either sides of the room. Their once sunken eyes had retreated completely into their skulls.

At the hotel, they found Winks in the courtyard bar. He had grown his hair long and was wearing wide glasses, a black knee length tailored coat, flares and stacked heels. The locals mistook Elias for a priest and requested his blessing which he gladly and grandly performed. Jamie spent a few days with them talking, drinking and laughing in a celebratory mood. Winks, as usual, was mostly quiet. They gorged themselves at seafood restaurants, visited a wax museum and hired a car to visit the pyramids of the Sun and the Moon. On a balcony high above the city Elias drew a circle in the air. "Your mission continues here."

Part One

The air shimmered and Elias was gone. There, below, was the French Quarter of New Orleans and the Mississippi River. Jamie descended in an antique cage of an elevator and strolled through the French Quarter to an old bar.

A few days later, at a club just off Bourbon Street, Jamie flirted with one of the talented dancers; a blonde with friendly green eyes and a trim athletic body. She invited him to the back where smudged and streaked mirrors lined a hallway. A rare and intoxicating smell of musk, bleach, cigarette smoke and alcohol fumes drifted through the place. Monotonous rock music pounded through the walls. In a small room that was a study in tawdry furnishings and bad housekeeping the blonde dancer rubbed her naked buttocks against his crotch. Jamie pulled her to him. "Do you have a hundred dollars?" she asked as her hand crawled into his pants.

The next day at a diner Jamie tucked a piece of pecan pie into his mouth and read his horoscope. That night he packed and took to the road. By train, bus and car, spending countless nights in hotels, motels and—rooms, he crisscrossed the land eventually ending up in Harrisburg, Pennsylvania by the Susquehanna River. Jamie checked into the elegant Hotel Red Star. On the terrace a pile of paperbacks covered a table. One, with a faded jacket drew his attention: skull men embedded into a wall, exposed to some Arctic landscape of space. "The Book of The Other, The New Species" by Dr. Adam Hunter, Ph.D.

Two Committee agents came into the hotel bar. One was black, the other white. Whitey was tall, lanky and wore a wide brimmed leather hat and long leather coat like a Spaghetti Western heavy. The black was shorter, quiet in a running outfit, and moved like he was grooving to some funky Caribbean rhythm. Asshole written all over their stony Committee faces. They reminded Jamie of the two identically dressed twins that had tried to stop him back in the Tenderloin in San Francisco.

They took seats on either side of him. Jamie finished his drink and tried to ease off the stool when Whitey patted him on the back, almost caressing it, then held his hand there firmly.

"Don't be in a hurry, Jamie boy. Let us buy you another. Isn't that right, Walker?"

"Yeah, muthafucka, let us buy you another drinky poo."

Walker's breath was foul, maybe toxic. Jamie closed his eyes and saw traces of the red light. Jamie stayed with the light until it grew and filled up his head. A gun was there in his hand. Jamie was across the room and in slomo the two Committee boys were going for their guns. Walker mouthed "He's hip. He's in the dream," but Jamie fanned off multiple shots that reduced them to headless, bubbling stumps. Walker's hand twitched as though to grasp for the automatic that had fallen just an inch from it. Whitey's gun remained in his waist holster and his pants were wet from urine. The bartender and other patrons had long vanished.

A Chinese man appeared in a squashed straw hat with a mouthful of metal. He handed Jamie his drink, which had turned into something resembling blood. Jamie drank it and stepped out into the night. Mist fell under the bright yellow lights of the street lamps that seemed to be slowly melting above him. Elias's face was before him, enormous and golden. Winks idly plucked at a sleeve in the flickering light of an errant street lamp.

Anna laid on the bed in Jamie's hotel room; light from the TV playing over her bare legs. Jamie listened. There was a tap on the door; he opened it to a square of black liquid. A ball of hazy light floating within. The light was Elias's face. A white beam shot upwards out of his right eye and the room lit up like a hundred flash bulbs had just popped. Then Elias was in the room taking off his hooded robe.

"Time is coming, Jamie." A little smile appeared at the corners of his mouth.

"And there's still time?" Anna asked sleepily.

* * * * * *

Washington, D. C. The Committee's weekly meeting. In an anonymous gray chamber an image was projected onto a screen. A square with an eye in the middle.

"They're sorcerers, not necromancers like us," a black senator said to a group of twenty-one.

"No. The difference is," a liver faced congressman spoke, "they're devils whereas we are in the Army of our Lord." He theatrically made a bowl of his hands.

The General, with snarling agents in black suits and watch caps on either side, chuckled. Gods and devils, he laughed to himself. It sounded like the goddamned Middle Ages.

"There was the nonaggression treaty we signed," an older cabinet member stated with a tightness in his voice.

The chairman, a Southern son wearing a shiny purple cape suit, stood and his face clouded. He turned hateful eyes on the cabi-

Part One

net member. As he spoke he made little chopping motions with his hand and sucked the air through his teeth.

"We are the Committee and don't you ever forget, you idjit." He turned to his right. "Doc," he snapped, "what the fuck is the story?"

The doctor, wearing a white smock and thick glasses looked up from his papers. His mouth was a permanent frown. A herpes simplex sore by his lower lip.

"Well..." he began uncertainly, "we don't have a reliable read on any of them as yet, but that gives us more time to continue the investigation." He coughed into his hand. "And it'll all be delegated to the back channels and the feeders."

An energetic boyish senator, obviously not satisfied, stood. "Gentlemen, I've been examining this file thoroughly. And it's been growing since the excavation. Although all the witnesses saw something, the capsule was empty when our people arrived. Since then there's been a number of other sightings. Elias is a suspect in a double homicide, though it's true we have no current status on him."

The Chief, who had been listening quietly and brooding, removed a pair of dark glasses and glared across the room. He wore a loud turquoise turtleneck under a black jacket. He drew a square in the air. An aide handed him another glass of white wine. Someone hissed in the back and someone else stifled a laugh. The senator looked around to confront his critics but at first no one said anything.

"What of the rumor that Elias and his gang are merely petty criminals who have since fallen into the legion of the homeless?"

"And their exploits?"

"Fictions of desperate agents that have lost their minds?"

"That is simply not so."

The senator continued. "Last sighted in Mexico but have since disappeared, as well as everyone connected with that group." The senator cleared his throat. "Our men there appear to have been stopped." The Chief looked down at his drink. The black ravenous eyes of the General scanned the room. There was a murmur of voices in the gray chamber.

The black senator drew a square and said, "I understand Elias may be the liaison?"

"Yes," the boyish senator answered, a note of confidence in his voice. "The beloved Enemy confirms."

Part Two

FIVE

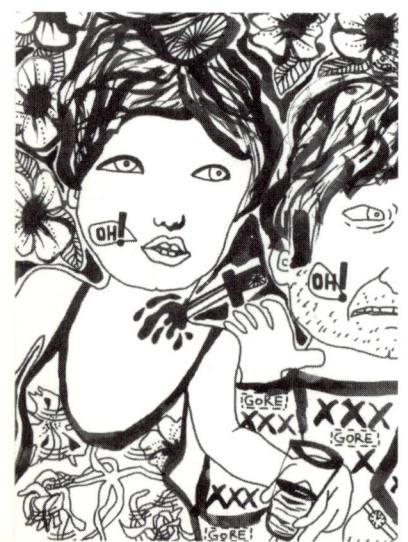

Tweety Bird squinted behind the wheel of the stolen Oldsmobile that cut through the morning fog. The smoke from his cigarette was getting in his eyes and he cursed as he drove by a derelict warehouse area where people roasted animals on barbecue pits in vacant lots.

He noted all the wrecked cars and buses up on blocks, and how everything was overgrown with a faintly glowing vine.

A group of men with shotguns resting in the crooks of their arms appeared from behind a building and walked towards a pit fire where women with rollers in their hair stared blankly into the flames. Tweety circled back, noting a few spots that could serve as future hideouts.

The engine coughed and died. He pulled over, cursed, got out and kicked the doors. Hostility swam through him like some deadly sea creature. He was at least three miles from the city and he blamed the car, the city and God. He opted to abandon the stolen car and walked off.

In the city's outskirts he stopped at an old house and crept up to a window by some bushes to look in, hoping to see some sex act or at least a naked person. Instead he saw an old man at a table bent over a bowl of soup. Tweety banged on the window and the old man knocked over his soup. Tweety Bird pressed his lips and nose to the glass and squished them around. Horrified, the old man watched him. Tweety laughed at the old man, took a leak and then walked on. Later, he rested on a bench, alone in a spacious arena. A greenish glow seemed to seep into his mind from distant antechambers before turning into a vast black ocean that engulfed him in sleep.

When Tweety Bird awoke he was surrounded by a group of white haired oldsters. Some of them were in wheelchairs, others on walkers. They peered at him through thick glasses with slanted, toothless expressions. He got up, looked around and blinked. He was in the courtyard of a nursing home. He spotted a bar across the street.

In the shabby bar Tweety Bird wrapped his mouth around a bottle of beer. The faces in the half dark looked like melted rock formations to him. Blue neon glared through a window, then dimmed, then glared and Tweety became mesmerized. He started to toss down shots of bourbon with his beer. When Tweety had too much to drink he became overly polite. He tried to curb his drinking but generally failed. Thorton Blankenship, Tweety's real name, found himself leaving. Then he had to piss again. He envisioned a clean men's room in the upscale restaurant that was across the street. People seemed to be floating. Tweety floated with them.

He held the door for a well dressed black man who looked irritated. The man was displeased at having received his steak overcooked. Tweety grinned idiotically and the black man sneered.

Tweety lurched into the bathroom, weaving slightly in front of a fat man with a purple face wearing a purple suit. The man looked at him dully, seeing Tweety only as an obstacle. Tweety bowed and mumbled some excuse. This only prompted the purple man to push by. Tweety fell against the wall, uttered a plea of forgiveness and felt his stomach turn over.

In the busy hallway, the pur-

PORTS OF HELL

ple man farted and headed back to the table of boozed up out-of-town salesmen.

A faraway look came over Tweety Bird and then he vomited in the urinal filled with cracked ice. He vomited some more and then he went to the sink to wash his face.

On the walk back to his crummy room, a jaywalking Tweety Bird was clipped by a car. A paramedic van was parked nearby and the men in it threw their sandwiches back in their bags and went to his rescue.

* * * * * *

Two months later, Tweety Bird escaped from the hospital. His tibia had mended as well as the hernia and other abrasions he had suffered. Pale from no sun, he wandered the city streets like a ghoul.

He stopped to gather the material of the stolen pants. He had rolled up the legs but the waist was almost two sizes too large. There was no belt. Tweety had made a rubber band belt but had somehow lost it. The first thing on his agenda was to find some clothes that fit.

The hospital had been fairly easy to escape from, but the only available clothes were those of the attendant, who was two sizes larger.

He had bided his time, waited for the right moment and then made an easy escape. Now he let the city wash over him. He welcomed it and let it seep into his mind. He picked up on the noises returning like a tune to his sensitive ears. He hummed an aria from an opera he had heard somewhere.

Tweety found a man who looked his size and began to shadow him. The man headed through Golden Gate park. As the man rounded a corner, Tweety stepped out from behind a tree and slashed his throat with a scalpel. The blood filled the man's lungs as Tweety held him and dragged him back into some brush. He struggled with getting off the clothes. Tweety changed, glancing around and maneuvering the body back behind some thicker bushes. He checked the pockets. $121, keys, wallet with license and three credit cards, a half a pack of peppermint breath savers and a used handkerchief that he pulled out with two fingers and let fall to the ground. He walked out of the park and flagged a cab.

Tweety looked at the old residence hotel that was the address on the license. The man had lived on the nineteenth floor. Tweety figured he was a bachelor since he wore a school ring rather than a wedding band.

Part Two

Tweety approached the entrance; no one was around.

A repugnant swarthy man rushed out and Tweety grabbed the door without the man even noticing. Tweety made for the elevator and ascended to the nineteenth floor. He knocked at the door and no one answered. The third key let him in. He turned on a light to reveal a basic bachelor studio.

After a shower, he helped himself to some fruit and a glass of milk. He put on some fresh clothes: his had blood on them. He cased the apartment and, before long, found himself $400 richer.

Tweety Bird decided to take a nap. He lay there on the couch, blinking. Everything seemed to be floating again. His reflection in a cloudy mirror made him appear Chinese. He entered the mirror and found himself in a smoky room. He watched a muscular woman devour three chocolate éclairs. She gazed at him with a chocolate covered smile.

Other people appeared out of smoke: barflies that kept changing seats. One against a wall, eyes shut in a stupor, poured himself an imaginary drink and ate an imaginary meal. Then he saw the floating policemen and he jumped up into blackness. Tweety awoke to find that he was back in prison. Donuts was there too. A dull pain spread from the back of his skull through his entire body.

* * * * * *

The desk clerk opened and shut his mouth as though manipulated by some invisible puppeteer. Jamie disappeared into the dark elevator with the rent receipt.

Jamie was staying at this forgotten old hotel in Chinatown with an alleyway entrance. His had a job at the Transition Center as a clerk. His job duties: updating files and giving referrals to the released prisoners of the California penal system. The Committee had access to the Transition Centers files and now so did Elias.

In the early morning Jamie climbed to the top of a hill where the view of the buildings below resembled giant dominoes. He watched his bus move slug-like up the hills amidst red, green and yellow blinking traffic lights. Once at the office, Jamie turned on a lamp. His desk was littered with stacks of written reports, files in various states, a desk calendar, a dirty bone-colored phone, two paper clip holders, a snake plant in a copper colored pot that was also sprouting a new lighter colored plant. Jamie bit into a jelly donut and sipped coffee through the plastic lid. Gradually he began to sort out the pile of work on the desk. The day passed, he punched out and walked back to the hotel. After being cooped up all day Jamie preferred walking to riding the crowded buses. He had been undercover now for two months. He made weekly reports to Elias, who listened quietly and occasionally had him elaborate. When Jamie complained about the mundaneness of the task he would be reminded that most intelligence work was mundane. In his room, Jamie had a cup of tea and put in the call. Just up from a nap, Elias's voice was thick over the phone. "Hang on Jamie. The dream invasion continues. Something will break."

And it did. The following day. Jamie scanned all the new intakes on a computer. He found what he was looking for and put holds on Douglas McDonough and Thorton Blankenship, a.k.a. Donuts and Tweety Bird.

Jamie read the reports. As his name suggested, Donuts was a big eater, carrying nearly 320 pounds. In the first photograph Donut's green eyes seemed to radiate a peculiar menace. But in his second photo he had a smile like a sweet little boy.

Tweety Bird was a wiry, rail of a man with a vicious serpentine look to him and an off-kilterness in his dark brown eyes. Under mannerisms humming was listed. It was noted that Tweety used to have a high voice, hence the monicker, but when the voice had changed the nickname had not.

Jamie read that Donuts favored loud, flowing shirts and in both pictures wore a garish yellow one covered with lime green pineapples.

In Tweety Bird's photos he was unshaven and wore a greasy looking jean jacket. He had the eyes of a bad acid tripper or meth head. Jamie read through the charts. Amusingly, the previous interviewer had diagnosed Donuts as "bipolar and narcissistic," and Tweety Bird as suffering from "low self-esteem issues." Their crimes were numerous and violent.

The Committee combed the state prisons for usable material and would arrange for an early release through the Transition Center, or TC.

Both these men were tagged by the Committee. There was a red star in the lower left corner of the cover pages. Jamie knew that once their purpose was served they were quietly eliminated. The very loyal and successful did manage to stay on in the service of the Committee: on a lowly level, but that beat the alternative. Donuts, having angled them this opportunity, understood this

Part Two

implicitly and it was his objective to stay on. He tried to explain it to Tweety Bird at the halfway house and, although Tweety nodded, the frowns indicated to Donuts that he either didn't get it, or that he wasn't too interested. Donuts sipped a chocolate milk with a cartoon rabbit on the carton and squinted at Tweety who was slouching in a stuffed, grimy chair and staring out the window.

"Tweety, we're out of the joint and if we play our cards right we'll stay out and work for the Committee."

Tweety coughed, glanced around, "Yeah, but it's government. I don't trust the government. In fact," he looked around the room, "we could be bugged now." Donuts sighed. "We already checked it out, remember? Everything's cool. Please."

Tweety turned back to the window and began to hum some unknown ditty. Donuts finished off his milk. "Tomorrow we go to the TC, get our papers cleared and get our funny money. The Committee man is coming by on Saturday."

The following morning Tweety Bird sat across from Jamie. Jamie felt his manic energy and proceeded slowly with the intake.

"What kind of job do you think you're suited for?" Jamie asked. Tweety shrugged but broke the silence that followed with, "Well, I used to be a swamper, so maybe I could learn to be a barkeep."

Jamie knew that a swamper was just somebody who mopped up the bar with a rag, collected empties and cleaned out the ashtrays. A job for a lush that was usually paid in drinks only. "But you said that you don't drink," Jamie said looking over the preceding page of the report.

Tweety coughed. "Well, I gave it up see. If I drink I get like some other person, real soft and squishy and then I get sick. I quit the sauce 'cause I like to keep my edge."

"But wouldn't you be tempted to drink as a bartender?"

Tweety looked confused. "Well, I don't know. What other kind of job can you get me?"

"I can't get you any job, Thorton." Jamie tapped his top teeth with his pen. "I can only get your papers cleared, give you a voucher for your money and give you some referrals where you might pick up something like handing out leaflets, or minor cleanup work at some construction sites."

Tweety frowned and asked if he could go.

He signed the remaining releases.

Donuts' intake was to be done at ten o'clock and Jamie decided that he was the one to shadow.

PORTS OF HELL

Donuts showed up right on time, dropped his weight onto the chair, blew his nose and said, "Okay, what do you need to know? I have a busy day ahead of me."

Assuring Donuts he would get him through the intake as quickly as possible, Jamie began asking the usual questions. When he got to the section that listed medical problems, Donuts complained about all his ailments, real and imagined. He seemed to hold the world at large somehow responsible.

Jamie gave him an MD referral but Donuts harrumphed, put the card in his shirt pocket and said, "Haven't met a doctor yet that was any damn good." Donuts, too, signed all the releases. Both he and Tweety had given different addresses on the same street. As soon as Donuts left, Jamie called the receptionist and told her he was going out.

Donuts made his way along Polk Street heading towards the bay. Jamie stopped to buy a drink, keeping him in sight. At Clay Street, Donuts moved at a fair speed, heading for the No. 1 California bus. It would be too obvious to board. There was no second bus in sight.

Jamie flagged a cab. It was driven by a Hispanic man with salsa blasting from his radio.

"Follow the bus," Jamie said over the music. The driver turned it down a tad and looked at him in the rearview mirror. "I'm an inspector," Jamie said to his eyes and flashed a bogus-yet-impressive badge when the cabbie turned around. "We've gotten a report that this driver only stops when he feels like it."

"Yeah huh, you gonna bust hez ass?"

"Let's wait and see." The bus pulled over at the next stop. The cab hung back and ignored the horn blowing of an agitated yuppie at the wheel of a metallic blue Volvo.

Donuts got out on Stockton Street and headed towards a Chinese bakery. Jamie gave the cabby a tip and acted like he was writing his number down. Donuts loaded up with a hefty array of cakes and pies, then waited for the downtown Stockton bus.

Jamie knew he would have to board to keep up with him. On the bus, it was apparent that Donuts was oblivious that he was being shadowed. They passed through the Stockton tunnel and arrived downtown. Jamie stayed behind as Donuts made his way down Market Street. Finally Donuts entered a mean looking rooming house on Turk Street.

The old building held Jamie's attention for a while. He had lived there years ago. In the

Part Two

building's early history, DALT had been painted on its side near the top. Over the years it had faded and a section at the top had been repainted. Now the top of the T was gone and it looked more like DALI.

Tweety Bird came out of an adult arcade a block away. He had an insane leer on his face. He turned in the direction of the old rooming house. An Arab dressed in work clothes, with a lightning bolt scar down his bony, left cheek, stood by the entrance. He carried a newspaper rolled tightly as though he had been worrying over something.

There was a high screech and metallic thud and across the street a red sports car was now lying on its side. A front tire spun. A police car with flashing blue-and-red lights pulled in by the smashed in taxi, its dome light now on the hood. The neighborhood was gaudy and unpleasant and its denizens gathered around the wreckage.

* * * * * *

The General of the Committee sat in his off-white office frowning at a computer screen. The walls were lined with files. The ceiling was extremely high. Directly above was a rectangular sky light. The General had short, gray, receded hair and black eyebrows in need of a trim. He had the pale, animal eyes of the Committee. The General was eighty-four, yet had the body and energy of a man half that age. He typed something into his computer and under his breath said: "Let's get on with it then."

* * * * * *

Early Saturday morning Jamie talked briefly on the phone with Elias. An hour later, at a 1950s Americana theme diner, Jamie ordered coffee. He looked around at the jukeboxes, old radios and an Edsel which had finally found its resting place in the back of the room, its parking lights blinking. Elias appeared across from him wearing a white turban, white shirt and a white sweater. He held a pearl handled cane.

"What a curious place," Elias said, looked around. "Let's hope the food is good." They sopped up their eggs with toast and drank coffee. When they finished, Elias wiped his mouth with a napkin, smiled and showed his tiny sparkling teeth.

"It's true," Elias said. "McDonough and Blankenship have been given their assignments. They've been ticketed through to Sri Lanka. They're to assassinate a British writer there. This person is not directly connected but sympathetic and has

PORTS OF HELL

written a brief but surprisingly accurate exposé on the Committee. It will hardly be read except in the underground presses, but the Committee wants her stopped. And in Sri Lanka, it's easy for a person to simply disappear."

Elias snapped open his briefcase and shuffled tickets, the aforementioned paper and some brochures across the table. Jamie turned to signal the waiter who stood in front of a huge bulbous faced jukebox. When he turned back Elias had disappeared.

The materials went into Jamie's wool blazer pocket. Out on the street it was a cool December morning. He wouldn't be needing any wool in Sri Lanka, the teardrop shaped island near the tip of India.

The usual drunks, pill heads, SSI collectors and petty criminals stumbled about in the early morning, lighted butts and blinked. "Spare change?" Fifteen minutes later Jamie was back in his room. He had ten hours to kill before boarding the flight which would make stops in Taipei and Bangkok. Jamie packed, put the room in order and laid down for a nap.

7:00 P.M. On Market Street Jamie stopped at the nearest tourist hotel to sign up for the Super Shuttle. It had turned even colder and the fog had moved in. He shivered. Tourists came out of the hotel, signaled cabs or walked briskly away to cocktails and dinner.

At the airport Jamie took a seat. Across from him an older man in a straw cowboy hat sat talking with an elderly Asian woman. In another area Jamie spotted Donuts wearing a garish shirt that featured zig zags of orange, black and red. Tweety Bird sat next to him wearing a baseball hat that read "Great America." The hat's bill bent into an upside down U. Tweety held two coffees and handed one over to Donuts.

Donuts sipped his creamy coffee and looked over the cup at Tweety. "It's much wiser for me to handle our cash. We haven't even converted into rupees yet."

Tweety turned sulky, bit the brim of the cup and caught the eye of an old lady who was idly watching them. "The fuck you looking at bag face?" The old lady quickly looked away. Without missing a beat Tweety said, "I feel funny not having a damn dollar on me and I hate asking for chump change."

"Tweety, remember in the joint? How I handled all our currency? Were you ever wanting? I ask you."

Tweety said no but that still he would feel better with some cash in pocket. Donuts sat his coffee down and forked over some

Part Two

money. "There, and as soon as we've converted to the rupee and as soon as you understand the money difference, I'll give you your share. Fair enough?" Tweety said okay and looked back at the old lady who continued to stare intently at the floor.

Jamie's seat on the plane was next to the old guy with the straw cowboy hat. The old cowboy smiled and promptly introduced himself as Bob Malloy. He had yellow teeth that protruded in front but didn't have any in the back. This reminded Jamie of an old horse. Once the plane had leveled off Malloy was quick to order his first screwdriver. He asked Jamie what he did for a living and Jamie told him he was a writer.

Malloy's face lit up.

"Well, I'm going to enjoy sitting next to you," he said. "Many people have told me that I should write a book about my life, or have someone else write it."

The plane climbed some more. Malloy tasted his screwdriver and settled back to tell his story.

He was born in the Ozarks and his father was a 'son of a bitch' who 'beat the shit out of him.' Malloy ran away at age thirteen and hitched a ride to Los Angeles. Before long he landed a job as a pin boy at a bowling alley where they let him sleep.

A few years later, he drifted into construction work and then, on a whim, enlisted in the air force. Jamie wondered how Malloy had gotten the education required to train as a pilot.

When Malloy couldn't find the stewardess for a refill he rustled through a bag at his feet and came up with a bottle of peppermint schnapps. He took a couple of slugs and put it back. He complained about stomach trouble, made a sour face and excused himself to go vomit in the bathroom.

When Malloy returned, he told Jamie he was afraid he had stomach cancer. He said the doctors had done a colonoscopy and had found nothing wrong, but they hadn't checked for stomach cancer yet. Malloy felt fairly certain that was what he had.

The stewardess appeared and Malloy promptly ordered another drink. He returned to his story. As a pilot, he had crashed twice and had never really recovered. His back had never been right since. Jamie could see him: a younger, leaner Malloy crawling out of the cockpit, dazed, looking around, wiping his brow and saying "Gawd damn," or something.

Malloy said that after the second crash he had come to in a hospital in Italy. The Hemingwayesque saga continued with a boxing story. Malloy said he had been a fair middleweight. He was stationed on a carrier. A champion middleweight was coming to the ship to give an exhibition. The champion was looking for someone to go a couple of rounds with. The other men talked him into it and he began training. The big day finally arrived and he walked into the ring to meet this famous boxer.

The conversation—or words—Malloy and the champion had went something like this: "I don't want to hurt a champion so I won't hit ya' hard." The champion: "That's 'cause you're scared."

When the champion winked, Malloy threw a left jab that caught him right on the button and knocked him out for the count. Malloy was carried on the shoulders of the laughing, cheering men and they celebrated riotously. He heard that when the champion had come to he swore he would kill Malloy.

As though Jamie had requested it, Malloy next began to list all the surgeries he had endured. Jamie barely followed it; a good part of him was drifting away into a little nap. Then the food arrived and Jamie woke up hungry. Malloy looked at his food and frowned.

"Can't keep anything down," he said.

Couldn't be all those screwdrivers and swigs of schnapps, Jamie thought and dove into the teriyaki chicken. Malloy tried a bite but then set his tray on the floor and headed off to the bathroom. He returned saying he had thrown up again. Malloy handed the stewardess his tray and ordered another drink.

Malloy was headed for the Philippines to see his bride to be. He talked about how much he loved her and how beautiful she was and Jamie became nauseated as he got all sappy and goo goo. "Oh, you should see her eyes and I know just what she'll say and what I'll say in return—" Malloy, Jamie discovered, like so many people, was only interested in himself. There was a typhoon currently pounding the Philippines and Malloy's new bride-to-be was on some obscure island. Malloy was overly concerned about her and said that if he couldn't get to that island he would steal a plane if need be.

At the Taipei airport Jamie was issued a new boarding pass. Donuts and Tweety Bird got theirs too. A limping Malloy was led off by a Chinese attendant. He called out to Jamie, "I'm sick. Gotta spend the night here." The waiting area reminded Jamie of some depressing, futuristic church, all white seats on one side and red on the other. Jamie slouched on the red side while Donuts and Tweety Bird dozed

Part Two

contentedly on the white side.

Jamie, Donuts, Tweety and the other passengers landed, in the middle of the night, in Bangkok. Jamie watched Donuts and Tweety Bird shuffle off towards a small restaurant. Jamie checked into a spiffy airport hotel and took a hot shower. Afterwards he munched on the complimentary fruit and switched the channels on the TV. He called the front desk and instructed them to wake him in six hours.

SIX

His name was Dan Roscoe and he was a private investigator. His turf was Miami's South Beach. Roscoe had a small seedy office behind an appliance store. He worked locally but occasionally got referrals and traveled. He attracted work due to his reputation of being discreet and honest.

It was another humid day and his office felt overly claustrophobic, he decided sourly. The AC was on the blink and, in spite of his overhead revolving fan, Roscoe wiped a bead of sweat off his forehead.

The phone rang. He picked it up and a male voice asked, "Mister Daniel Roscoe?"

"Yes, this is Dan Roscoe."

"This is Sonny Shields of Shields, Shields and Shields in New York City."

There was silence and so Roscoe said, "Yes?"

"I have some nice work for you Mister Roscoe. A substantial fee and a bonus if you can recover a stolen artifact and some money."

Roscoe thought of his only current job, the conspiracy obsessed Vietnam vet.

"I'm on a job but I'll be wrapping it up very soon."

The voice said, "Listen Mister Roscoe when I say piece of change I mean piece of change. We're one of the most prestigious investment firms in the country, we attract—"

"When?" Roscoe cut in.

"Immediately."

The voice from New York City gave him an address.

In the Miami airport a zoo of characters milled around: old Italian gangsters decked out in 1950s fedoras, pointy toed shoes and loud satin shirts; businessmen who looked more like suit salesmen stood around and ate junk food; Haitians dressed entirely in black sipped Cuban coffees, their women shapely and saucily outfitted and flashing white teeth; weirdo oldsters, never to be outdone, looking like models for thrift stores run by speed freaks.

PORTS OF HELL

Roscoe felt the humidity of the airport was not much better than his office, where the AC worked within the confines of its own cruel logic. He finished off a potboiler during the flight. At JFK he found a cab and checked into a small hotel in the Lower East Side.

The following morning Roscoe gave the cab driver an address in the Avenues. At an anonymous office building he got out of the cab and went inside. He took the computerized elevator to the thirty-seventh floor and found 3703. Behind a semi-circle of a desk, a mod beauty talked into a headset and appraised him with calm brown eyes.

Roscoe wore a gray gabardine suit, crisp white shirt and a maroon tie that gave off just a hint of gold. He was tan, as always, and fit from a previous job that had him racing all over the Caribbean. Her eyes found his.

"Dan Roscoe," he said and extended a hand.

She put her hand in his and he explored it: clean nails, gold signet ring. Their palms caressed and she smiled with a hint of seduction.

"You have awfully pretty hands," Roscoe said, giving it back to her.

"Thank you," she said, turning up her smile.

"I have an appointment with Sonny Shields."

She looked down at a leather bound, appointment pad and pressed a few buttons on a control board. "Mr. Shields? Yes, Mr. Roscoe is here, sir."

Roscoe was escorted down a hallway by offices where people blinked at their computer screens. His escort was an androgynous fellow in a green suit and a green shirt.

In a cavernous office, he found Sonny Shields pouring a cup of coffee. He offered some. Shields also held a fat cigar but he did not offer one of those.

He looked to be in his mid-fifties, fleshy faced, paunchy, gray hair cut too short and high on his fat head making him look like a nazi. His dull eyes completed the picture.

He offered a limp handshake. "Have a seat, Roscoe," he said.

Roscoe sat in a leather designer chair with no arms. Shields waved his cigar in front of him then slid it into a glass ashtray the size of a soup bowl. One end was slick with his saliva; it looked obscene laying there. A plume of blue smoke rose and formed a startling apparition. A curvaceous woman hung there for just a moment. Hallucination? Shields was oblivious but Roscoe was entranced.

"Sal, the youngest of my brothers and the third owner of this

Part Two

company, has flipped his ever loving wig," Shields said. "He's taken private cash savings, as well as an ancient, mystical artifact believed to belong to a civilization before the Egyptians."

"Atlantis?"

"Yes, or Lemuria,' he said dodging through the remaining smoke. "There's different theories. And there's the five million. We want what's left and the relic. We won't prosecute but we'll want him to sign a paper holding him to a set allowance for the rest of his life. And we must have the disk."

"The disk?"

"Yes it's a silver disk."

Shields plucked his cigar out of the ashtray and stuck it back into his mouth.

"What's the significance of this disk?"

The shift in his eyes told Roscoe he wasn't going to tell him. "We don't know yet," he said sniffing at his cigar. "But I understand you're one of the best, Roscoe. Find him, and retrieve what's left of the money and take five percent."

"Ten percent," Roscoe said flatly.

"Okay ten," Shields said and made Roscoe think he should have said fifteen.

"Fifteen," Roscoe said anyhow.

Shields nodded. "Okay, fifteen."

"When was Sal last seen?" Roscoe asked to get away from the topic of money. Sonny stepped over to a window that looked over the skyline of gray buildings. He let some smoke out of the side of his mouth. "Almost two weeks ago. At the end of the day he just fucking disappeared."

"Who else knows?"

"Just my other brother Stan. You want to talk to him?"

"Maybe later."

"We've told everybody else that Sal's on vacation."

"Keep it that way."

Sonny Shields bit on a lip, gave Roscoe his unlisted number and a key to Sal's office. Then he went back to staring out his window. Roscoe got the feeling he did a lot of that. Like Sonny's office, it was at the end of a private corridor. Roscoe let himself in and flipped on the light.

The blinds were down. Roscoe opened them and looked at the view, slightly inferior to Sonny's. On the bookcase were three framed photos of women. At first he thought they were all the same woman: long blonde hair, large breasted and hungry, almost predatory, mouths. But when he looked closer he saw that they were all different.

Roscoe carefully went through Sal's calendar. Two weeks before he had neatly printed "Waikiki" in red, sideways in the margin. The drawers were full of the usual: business cards, stamps, cough drops, computer paper, loose change, old keys. Roscoe put a call into Izzy, his hacker, and copied some numbers and addresses from a notebook. He nosed around some more and found a torn out ad for a massage parlor in a hefty book on mysticism.

After some more eye action with the secretary at the front desk, Roscoe took the elevator back down to the lobby. His stomach seemed to arrive a few seconds after the rest of him. Back at the hotel he retrieved the voice mail from Izzy. The electronically altered voice said: "Mr. Salvadore Shields had booked and departed on United flight 737 to Honolulu twelve days ago. I should have a hotel for you within the hour."

* * * * * *

Jamie was one of the few other Westerners waiting to board the plane to Sri Lanka. Besides himself and the duo, the others were mostly journalists going over to cover the recently heated up longstanding war between the Tamil Tigers LATTE and the government. The government was Buddhist, the Tamils Hindu and backed by Hindu factions in India. The Tamils included the notorious "Black Tiger" suicide bombers who each carried their own cyanide capsule. The latest report had the government forces pushing north and hoping to take Jaffna any day.

The inflight movie was *Die Hard*. Tweety Bird especially enjoyed it and laughed and hooted throughout. At the Colombo airport, everyone was subjected to a through security check and all luggage was meticulously searched twice. Jamie overheard Donuts quizzing drivers about prices to the Galle Face hotel in downtown Colombo. Elias had thought they might go north to the beach town of Negomba.

Jamie kept the duo in sight while he talked with a tour guide who went into a spiel about resort package deals. While Jamie continued to say naa, one of the half dozen Sinha words he had taught himself, the guide said, "You know you have arrived at rain season. It used to be not rain now but then the world changed."

Once Jamie had seen the duo pull off he instructed his driver to follow them. He gave them plenty of time to check in and when he entered the grand Galle Face Hotel, reputed to be even older than The Raffles of India, it was dark and empty in the lobby.

Part Two

One of the boys took his bags and found someone to do the check-in. Jamie was directed into a large dim room occupied by tall wooden cabinets and antique, roll top desks. A forgotten gloom permeated the atmosphere. Three hotel boys stood by silently.

Jamie filled out the forms and produced a credit card and passport. He looked at the register and saw where McDonough had signed by their room number. He requested a room on the floor directly below. Jamie was given three elaborate receipts. A boy took him up a small, ornate elevator and down a long, wide, red carpeted hallway to his room.

The worn yet adequate room faced a promenade by the sea, banked by a wide block of muddy ground between it and the road. At that hour it looked enchanting; he would not see the mud till the morning light. Jamie undressed, turned off the AC, which he almost always found intolerable, and went to bed.

Donuts and Tweety Bird headed out in the morning. Jamie watched them from the window then went downstairs for breakfast. He found the verandah dining area that overlooked the beach and rough Indian sea. He had porridge and a pot of Ceylon tea. Squirrels ran across the lawn and up and down the palm trees. Large crows flapped about trying to steal bread off the tables. The waiters in red skirts, white buttoned jackets, distinguished and variously styled beards and mustaches shooed the crows away. Jamie felt this was an activity that would be repeated daily as long as the Galle Face stood.

After breakfast, Jamie wandered the looming hallways where hotel boys lurked, stepping out to unexpectedly mutter "Good morning sir" at every turn. They seemed to be everywhere so he decided against having a look in the duo's room. Jamie took a seat in the lobby behind an exhibit of an antique car that Prince Philip or somebody had brought to the island and hid himself behind a newspaper.

An hour later, the duo were back. They were approached by a small man who jumped out from behind a desk and vigorously tried to sell them on various tours and excursions.

Donuts waved him away and fanned himself with a straw hat. He wore another bold shirt: bright green and gold plants constituted a weird jungle. The background was faintly luminescent and smaller blood red flowers bloomed here and there. Tweety wore his crumpled Great America baseball cap backwards and a gray T-shirt that was even darker from his perspiration.

Jamie got into a cab in front of the hotel. The driver repeated the address he gave him. They made their way through streets thick with three-wheelers, army trucks, buses and other cabs. The city was divided into eight sections. The squalor in some neighborhoods hit Jamie like a psychic black hole. And the bleak office and apartment buildings which one could now find in even the most remote countries just added to the dreariness. Dark men in saris walked barefoot by sandbags piled in front of impressive buildings. Soldiers armed with machine-guns stood unblinking at the entranceways.

It was reported the previous week that the rebels had set fire to a number of oil refineries in Colombo in retaliation for the government's push towards Jaffna. It was reputed that the rebels had executed a number of civilians in remote villages.

Blind and disfigured beggars wandered about. At a stoplight one with no hands approached the cab. He held his bowl out to the driver with his stumps and the driver dropped a few coins in. On a back street the driver asked an old lady a few questions. He acked up a few feet and pointed to a building. Jamie paid and told him not to wait. He went through a circular, overgrown courtyard and climbed a water logged wooden stairway.

At the top floor Jamie knocked and heard a muffled feminine voice. The door opened to a pretty, dark eyed, Sinhala servant girl with a broom in her hands. Behind her was a lady in her mid-twenties with shoulder length brown hair behind her ears, a clear complexion and big brown eyes that looked gold in the light. A couple of bottom teeth leaned just a touch to the side.

Jamie reached out a hand. "Jamie Coates," he said. "Your editor Mr. Richards said to look you up."

She smiled.

"Yes, of course. Come in please."

She said something in Sinha and the girl murmured and went off to a back room.

* * * * * *

A nervous twitch moved around Tweety Bird's sallow face. He sat on the bed and contemplated four fifty rupee notes in his hand. "Looks like fuckin' play money," he thought. Donuts came in and Tweety crumbled up the bills and stuck them in his pocket. Donuts had seen him but went straight into the bathroom. Donuts was still upset after complaining to the management.

Earlier, when he had lowered

Part Two

his large frame into the bathtub he had gotten a mild electric shock from the chain that held the plug. At first he had thought it was his imagination, but when he grabbed a hold of the side of the tub he got another and became frightened.

"What the fuck," he had yelled out to no one since Tweety had been out buying postcards. Desperate, Donuts had thought, "An electric shock and I'm in goddamn water!"

He foresaw the report from the embassy: "American tourist Douglas McDonough found dead in a bathtub at the Galle Face Hotel, Sri Lanka. Cause of death: electrocution." He had stepped out, careful not to touch anything, dried off and stared in disbelief at the tub as though it was some living entity that had tried to kill him. On the phone he had tried unsuccessfully to get the front desk so he had gone off in person to talk to somebody in charge.

The dusky Sinhala front desk manager listened unemotionally as Donuts conveyed his amazement and rage at being "electrocuted" by the bathtub. The front desk manager shook his head from side to side, apologized and said that a man would check his room. He offered Donuts a complimentary coffee. Donuts noticed that the Sinhalese did not shake their heads yes or no but rather sideways, reminding him of dashboard dogs. The damnedest thing, he thought, you can't tell if they're saying yes or no and this further infuriated him.

"To hell with the coffee." Donuts had said. "Fix the goddamn bathtub!"

Donuts, still upset, had stormed off to the terrace and ate a second breakfast. Afterwards he had half-heartedly leafed through some European newspapers attached to thin bamboo sticks and drank another pot of tea before returning to the room.

Now he ran some water in the bathtub and gingerly touched the chain; he touched the side. It had indeed been fixed, but he wasn't in the mood for a bath now. He looked at his pudgy, yellowish face in the mirror.

Suddenly, the sunlight that was coming through the window disappeared and it began to rain in torrential sheets. Donuts cursed and went into the bedroom to find Tweety again staring at the rupee notes.

"Thirty one rupees to the dollar. Don't you have it yet?" Donuts almost shouted.

"Yeah. I got it. But what about these?" Tweety said and held a variety of coins in his thin hand.

Donuts patiently pointed out what each was worth, but for one he had to check his guidebook

PORTS OF HELL

which caused Tweety to smirk with some satisfaction. Donuts sat on the bed and cursed the rain.

"We'll wait 'til this lets up before we check out the broad's place," he said to Tweety's back.

Tweety sat at the old wooden desk and tried to think of a note he could write to his mother and sister. He bit a thumbnail and tried to concentrate.

"Dear Mom, I am here in Sri Lanka, which is near India. I am on business, scouting for an import company in San Francisco."

Tweety borrowed this story from Donuts, who had told it to a nosy journalist on the plane. "Love. Thorton."

"Dear Sis—" but he didn't want to say the same damn thing to her since they would talk and compare cards. He bit the top of the pen and thought for a minute, then wrote; "Howdy from Sri Lanky Love Tweets."

He put the cards aside and browsed through a tourist magazine that had been left on the desk. With some psychic discomfort he considered a photograph of devil dancers. They posed weirdly and wore grotesque masks and garish costumes. Donuts had taken a sleeping pill and dozed contentedly to the sound of the dark rain.

* * * * * *

Trisha sipped tea and nibbled on a ginger nut biscuit. "A delightful, spicy bite and a favorite of many," it said on the package. Jamie decided to get to the point since she was fishing around about his visit.

"I don't know Mr. Richards, Trisha. It's the piece you wrote about the Committee."

"Yes?"

She looked at him now as though just seeing him for the first time. She set her cup down.

"Yes. I'm with Elias."

She stared at him a moment longer.

"You're part of Operation Sun Ray, aren't you?" She ran her tongue over her top teeth.

Jamie was becoming aroused by her mouth. She demurred and sat back in the chair.

"Yes, also known as Operation Red Mirror."

"Have you seen the emissaries?"

"Not yet, but I'm here to help you. You're in danger you know."

"From the Committee?" she asked soberly but with a tremble that she didn't try to hide.

"They've sent two characters fresh from the California penal system," Jamie said. "Their assignment is what's referred as a 'stop.' But I'm well ahead of them. There's a safe house in Hikkaduwa."

Part Two

Jamie brought the empty cup to his nose and smelled the tea leaves.

"Trisha, Elias will visit you there."

They sat in silence for some time, listening to the downpour that had begun. She brewed more tea. Jamie patted her bare, brown leg and she smiled bravely.

* * * * * *

Just a half day of tropical sunshine had turned Donuts' large nose bright red and brought out a half dozen glaring pimples on his greasy forehead. He examined these changes in the bathroom mirror and cursed. The rain continued to come down in dark sheets.

Tweety had bought a bottle of Arak and sat by the window. He began to hum "If You Ever Go to Trinidad," a tune that had stuck in his head ever since he heard it on the radio back in San Francisco.

Donuts meandered back into the room, having too late dabbed his nose with sunscreen. The phone rang and they both looked at it suspiciously.

Donuts picked it up. "Hello?... Hello?"

There was nothing at the other end, then somebody said, "Hello... Good-bye," and hung up.

Donuts rang the front desk. "Who just called here?"

"Nobody call here sir."

"Somebody just—oh never mind." Donuts hung up. "This place is screwy. Let's go try the buffet."

The mister nice guy smile was plastered all over Tweety's face. "What's wrong with you?" Donuts said, narrowing his eyes. "You're drinking. You know what happens to you." Donuts was irritated and his eyes got beadier. Tweety, already long gone, smiled helplessly. Donuts grabbed the bottle from his hands, spilling some on the floor.

"Yes sir," Tweety said; he never said sir and at first Donuts wondered if he was imitating one of the legion of obsequious hotel boys. But Donuts saw that, no, Tweety had simply had one too many and was now well away in mister nice guy land.

"Fuck. Just what we need."

"Whatever you say," Tweety put out with idiot sincerity.

"You might as well stay here; you won't be able to eat and it'll just be an embarrassment."

"Yes sir." Tweety bowed, burped and apologized some more.

Donuts frowned and left the room, grunting on his way out. Tweety looked for the Arak bottle but Donuts had wisely stuck it in his jacket pocket when

PORTS OF HELL

Tweety had been bowing like some seventeenth century footman. Tweety waltzed into the bathroom. Everything seemed wonderful: and he would do everything he could to keep it that way.

Then he looked into the mirror and got sick; he vomited in the old porcelain bathtub.

After running cold water over his head for almost five minutes he was mostly sober. He ran more water over his head and tried to imagine the sexy Brit writer tied up in her bed. He would have some fun before he killed her. He already knew he would be the one. Donuts wouldn't do a woman. Donuts would get them into the place then go raid the ice box while he was left to the dirty work. That was okay, Tweety thought. He liked the dirty work and the limey was a sexy piece, going by her picture.

Donuts was not pleased with the buffet. He found the food tasteless and not warm enough.

But then he discovered a newly arrived mobile cooking station. The cook, in a tall white hat, happily made fried egg hoppers with curry spices on the side.

Later Donuts moved on to the also newly arrived chocolate mousse tray. He decided he could easily eat a fair share of the mousse. The dark Indian waiters eyed him with awe and exclaimed their horror and admiration to each other but were jubilant when they saw he was finally finished, although he had eaten the entire pan of mousse.

One waiter looked sadly at the empty tray, since his habit was to have a portion at the end of a hard night of serving all the crazy foreign tourists.

* * * * * *

Jamie emptied the packet into the pudding and stirred it around. In the bedroom he examined the head he had developed with a melon and a wig. A blanket up to where a neck would be. A thick mosquito netting helped to blur the vision. He let himself out of Trisha's apartment. Across the street, at a cafe, he took up his vigil at a small table and had tea. The rain had finally let up and twilight dispersed its final moments. A three-wheeler pulled over by a bar and emptied the large frame of Douglas McDonough followed by the wiry Thorton Blankenship, who glanced about with an animated, nervous energy.

Purple and yellow lights began to blink atop the bar like a stage set coming to life. A wandering cow picked a banana peel from a puddle of garbage with its yellow teeth and ate it. Some pretty girls

Part Two

in spotless white blouses with bundles of sticks on their heads walked by barefoot. Donuts argued with the driver for a minute then forked over a few more rupees. A strange soundtrack came from the bar: a kind of yodeling and chant accompanied by mechanical drums and a sitar. A mysterious scent drifted through the damp streets.

Jamie had read Donut's and Tweety Bird's histories, filled with crimes of heinous and irrational violence. The intensity of Donuts' beady eyes and Tweety's feverish blue black eyes flashed in front of him. They were bumblers but could be lethal. He figured they would both be armed: knives most likely—at least Tweety, that being his weapon of choice. Jamie fingered the handle of an Indian fighting knife secure in one pocket as he watched them enter the building. He felt the handle of the blackjack reassuringly in another. Jamie gave them two minutes before he, too, went in.

As Donuts discovered the bowl of coconut pudding that Jamie had even taken the time to sprinkle with cinnamon, Tweety was eyeing the bogus head. The notion that something was askew flickered through his deranged mind but in one fluid movement Jamie stepped in and rapped him effectively behind the ear. He fell lifeless into Jamie's open arms. He taped his arms, legs and mouth.

Jamie crouched and counted off two more minutes on his watch then moved quietly into the kitchen. He found McDonough unconscious on the floor. Donuts was clutching the nearly empty pudding bowl. A peculiar, pinched look had formed on his fat face. There was a tap at the door and Jamie let Hector into the room. Hector was an Elias contact, a Mexican who was fluent in Thai, Cambodian, Malay, and Sinhala.

SEVEN

"Mister Roscoe. Mister Roscoe," The pretty, Hawaiian stewardess said as she gently woke him. "We're preparing to land."

Roscoe took off his jacket for the shuttle ride to the hotel. The familiar tropical climate clung to him. The mountains in the distance were draped in clouds and seemed to drift there in the darkness. Roscoe checked into a hotel a few blocks from the Waikiki Hana where Sal Shields was registered.

After checking in Roscoe went to a bar on the beach and ordered a nightcap. Under an umbrella with his drink that also was un-

PORTS OF HELL

der a tiny umbrella, Roscoe gazed into the near dark. He listened to the surf which caused, as it always did, a slight trance state. Nearby was a quiet group of pretty Japanese girls. Across the room, a noisy bunch of American tourists wearing leis proposed absurd toasts and laughed drunkenly. Somewhere, the tinkering of a piano ended an old Hawaiian love song. A few people on the upper level of the restaurant clapped lazily.

In the morning Roscoe sat in the lobby of the Waikiki Hana. He spotted Sal from his photo, not much different than Sonny except ten years younger. But something did not seem right about him.

Sal made his way through the lobby and went out. Roscoe followed. A bald, bespectacled man holding out his hat invited Sal to a makeshift altar thrown up in front of a sushi bar. Some very plain women in very plain dresses were already gathered to one side looking at the printed hymn sheets. It was Sunday and the missionaries on the islands of the Pacific everywhere were trying to stir up business. Sal Shields was not interested nor were many others.

Roscoe followed him to an outside restaurant on the beach. Roscoe tucked himself in at the crowded counter and attempted to get some coffee. He watched Sal begin reading from an old book he carried. Finally the beach bum bartender poured Roscoe a cup of hot Kona into a tiki mug.

People were already staking claim to patches of beach with garish towels, humble mats, coolers, water sports gear, loud umbrellas and assorted beach furniture. The beach bums that worked the surfboard and umbrella rental stands busied themselves setting up. Roscoe watched a drop dead blonde in a silver bikini enter the water with a board, climb on and paddle out to an ocean that mirrored the sky. Some children were playing in a shallow area of small wavelets, the water like turquoise there. Roscoe decided to forget Sal Shields for awhile. He thought about having some breakfast but decided to have a drink or two first.

Roscoe cut through the grounds of one of the big hotels done up in a jungle theme. He was confronted by a bearded beach bum with gloriously colored parrots on each arm. The man tried his best to convince Roscoe to have a polaroid taken with the birds but Roscoe kept walking.

Down a number of sun splashed streets, he finally found a bar that appealed to him. In-

Part Two

side he found a slight mildew smell, peeling paint and at least two cockroaches. This was a welcome change from the overly expensive bars along the beach. It was more than a little dingy and that was just fine with Roscoe.

The bartender had a handsome face except for a puggish nose. He wore a faded blue shirt covered with faded white palm trees. Roscoe thought that maybe he was a former boxer. There were a couple of Samoans at a table with diminutive drinks before them, like drinks from a doll house. The bartender was a haole but as dark as the Samoans. There was no one else in the place. Roscoe took the seat by a wall.

"What'll it be?"

"Dark beer?"

"We no have darky beer."

"A greyhound then, Smirnoff. Y'know, all vodka no pretense."

"Smirnoff," the barkeep repeated and went off to make the drink. When he delivered it he said, "Sorry I don't get up till now and in bad mood. Okay now." Had this dude been punched one too many times and now talked like an imbecile? Roscoe wondered. "I live here now eleven years. Punchbowl." Indeed, Roscoe thought. "Still don't know no Hawaiian. You?"

"No, I'm with you," Roscoe said and gave him the "hang loose" Shaki hand sign. The bartender smiled and made one too. One of the Samoans demanded more drinks and he moved away to oblige. Roscoe drank off half of his greyhound and then the barkeep was back.

"Only English," he said, "You looky for gals?"

"What?" He had seen Roscoe checking out a prostitute in vinyl hot pants sashaying by, speaking Japanese into a cell phone.

"Here looky looky," the barkeep said and reached under the bar and came up with a red scrapbook. Roscoe opened it to an array of photographs like you see in the display windows of downtrodden strip joints. Young women posed in sexy costumes, bikinis and lingerie. Some of the girls he found inviting and when he pointed to one the barkeep shook his head sadly. "No not her. I forgot to take her out. She no work no more." A blank look came over him as he took her picture from the book. "Another please," he urged and gestured to the book with his towel wrapped hand. Roscoe tapped the empty glass and the barkeep scooped it up and went off to make another. Roscoe browsed through the book. The bartender grinned when he saw Roscoe return again and again to one particular photo.

"How old?"

"Twenty-one, almost twenty-two now." Everything would be arranged. A necessary expense.

Two hours later Nora greeted him in the lobby. She was tan and fresh and had mischievous brown eyes.

"Do you want to see some ID Mr. Roscoe?"

"Dan please."

"Maybe I like calling you mister." She stroked his chin with an index finger.

"Call me what you like."

"That's better," she said triumphantly.

In the morning on the lanai, Roscoe watched her pour a cup of coffee and spread papaya jam on toast. Her hair was pulled back accentuating her features. She wore no makeup and as the cliché goes, "was even more attractive." She wore a short white towel around her waist and was all breasts and legs. They sipped coffee and munched toast. She kept crossing and re-crossing her legs and before long they were back in bed.

She asked Roscoe why he was in Hawaii and he told her he was a PI on a case. She was to leave later in the day on a weekend cruise to Maui with a group of Japanese businessmen.

"Picked from the photo book?" Roscoe asked with his most nonexpressive look but felt it still showed some disappointment.

"No darling, prearranged. Now come and join me in the shower." He opened the blinds and let the tropical sunshine fill the room.

* * * * * *

At dawn Donuts was the first to come to. He and Tweety Bird were naked and laying on the beach in Negombo. They had been bitten repeatedly by hordes of mosquitoes. Donuts let out a howl and pawed at the bites. Shocked, he drew back when he saw the wiry body of Tweety Bird in fetal position next to him in the sand. He roused Tweety, who awoke jerking his head about like a lizard. Tweety tried unsuccessfully to make some sense of the strange environment and state of affairs he found himself in.

"What the shit!"

"What the shit indeed," Donuts echoed, then doubled over and dry heaved.

"Jesus," Tweety said and grabbed his manhood and looked desperately for something to cover it with. Then he felt the bump on his head and a dull remote pain. Another, sharper, pain hovered around the base of his spine.

Donuts coughed. "Tweety, there's something wrong with my

Part Two

throat." He coughed again and when he spoke, he was hoarse. "It's in my lungs and ears, too!"

Tweety said, "It's okay. We've been beat but we're still kicking." He looked up and down the beach and laughed. "Donuts my man, we need some clothes unless this is a nudie beach." They scrambled back into some brush. When two native fishermen came down the beach with plastic bags full of the morning's catch they attacked them. The frenzied, bizarre fight that ensued ended with Tweety clubbing his victim with a piece of pipe and Donuts strangling his opponent, who gasped horribly before expiring. They dragged the bodies deeper into the brush and covered them with sand and weeds. Some of the fish had gotten out of the bags and flopped about in the sand.

The duo, wearing the red lunghis of the dead fishermen, came down the esplanade that fronted the brown, muddy, stretch of ground to the Galle Face. Donuts held his lunghis together, not being able to find enough material to tie it. Donuts had come to his senses but still whined about his sore throat and bites. He foolishly scratched with his free hand and spread the histamine and caused the bites to bleed.

After they had killed the fishermen, Donuts had almost screamed when he'd spotted a bumblebee the size of a baby's fist coming towards him. He'd cursed while Tweety snickered and said, "Let's get the fuck out of here Donuts." Tweety, in fact, had weathered the episode much better and even refused to scratch the bites. On the walk along the esplanade he looked forward to a hot shower and a handful of aspirin. He silently thanked himself for having packed them. He remembered what a top commodity aspirin had been in the joint. A handful chewed up, chased with a coke would give a man a bit of a buzz.

The rain started again and they were soaked before they reached the grand old hotel. The staff looked on in disbelief as the two dripping wet Americans in lunghis plodded through the lobby. The elevator man was so dumbfounded he did not offer them a ride. He knew he should have, but he was caught off guard by the spectacle.

The final straw for Donuts at the Galle Face came as he had just been starting to doze off. Water hit him right smack in the face. He jumped up and swore, which did not awaken Tweety. Donuts rustled him awake and pointed to the steady stream of water falling onto the bed. Tweety, with his bony fists tight as though to fight, saw the wa-

PORTS OF HELL

ter on the bed and thought for a wild moment that Donuts had pissed himself. Then he realized it was coming from the leaky roof.

"We're getting out of here now," Donuts proclaimed.

Earlier, they had received a cable from the Chief that instructed them to abandon the assignment and report back to San Francisco ASAP. At the front of the hotel with their bags in tow, they were mobbed by a horde of beggars, deformed invalids and assorted con men. A boy with his back against a wall played a flute and moved slightly from side to side charming a lazy snake out of the basket. Donuts wondered if he could charm them a cab.

A deaf-and-dumb man tried to get Donuts to donate money to the Deaf and Dumb Center. At first Donuts thought he was a cab driver since he wore a shirt, pants and carried a notebook, and he did end up procuring one.

Donuts told the driver to take them directly to the airport. Once there, they found that they couldn't get permission from the guard to go beyond a certain checkpoint. Finally, the driver convinced the guard, after a thorough search, to let them through. At the terminal, another guard would not let them take their bags inside and insisted that the taxi leave. After all that, they found the Thai Airways station closed.

At Air Lanka a bored clerk told them that the other airlines would not be open till morning and that there were no flights out until the following evening. They went back to collect their bags and, since there were no taxis, started to walk the couple of kilometers to an airport hotel. Wet from the pissing rain, they checked into a dreary airport hotel.

Low wattage bulbs were used in most buildings in Sri Lanka, giving places an overall dimness, and the airport hotel was no exception. Spotting the restaurant, Donuts instructed the bellboy to deliver the bags to the room, then to deliver the room key to them in one of the booths.

The only other customers were four Sinhala teenagers asleep with their heads on the table by empty coke bottles. Donuts squinted at the menu. Tweety said he would have the same, looking at the teenagers and wondered why they were sleeping there.

Something had happened when Tweety had taken the knockout with more savvy than Donuts: they had become more like equals. Nothing was ever said about it; but it had definitely occurred.

The meal that arrived was wet rice with a dark piece of fish and the inevitable potent curry. Donuts made a face but dug in.

Part Two

Tweety picked at it and said, "Jesus, Donuts, what'dya order here?"

"It's the only thing I could make out on the menu," Donuts whined.

"Well, you can have mine," Tweety said and pushed the plate away. He pulled out a candy bar and munched. Donuts gave the bar a brief wanting look before continuing to chow down.

As if following some pre-arranged sleepwalkers code, the teenagers all awoke, stood and filed out of the cafe. The waiter said something to them and one mumbled something back. Tweety wondered what they had said.

Their room was dark and contained a grimy wall-to-wall carpet as well as a general moldiness. When Donuts saw the mosquitoes, he went on a rampage with a newspaper. Tweety tried to get something on the TV. When Donuts was done, the walls were splotched with blood smears as though some diabolical rite had been performed. Tweety, snickering, watched an Indian soap opera. An exhausted Donuts looked wearily at the two blue mosquito nets whose shadows appeared like some incubated, otherworldly creatures. On the porch were two inches of water and the AC loud enough to wake the Deaf School of Colombo. Outside, crows gathered around a stagnant looking swimming pool. Their cawing, Donuts felt, was to remind him of the general bleakness that had hung over them the entire trip.

In the morning they rented a car with driver and went back into Colombo City to change tickets for a flight to Bangkok. Later in the day they checked out and, by cab, headed in the direction of the departure terminal. Almost immediately the cab got into a long, slow queue that had to pass a check point.

The driver tried to reassure them that the soldiers only wanted to check his permit, then would let them pass. But when they approached the checkpoint the soldiers who gripped machine guns slung on their shoulders shook their heads. The taxi driver spoke to one who answered but continued the side-to-side head shake that made Donuts crazy. The driver turned around and said, "You have to go to another place first. They just make this rule today."

Donuts, beside himself, yelped, "Our flight! Our flight!"

He desperately wanted out of this dark country full of rain, mosquitoes, a war he didn't understand and, even worse, bad food. He waved the tickets at the guard who continued to shake his head and point back the way they had come. The driver pulled out.

"Don't worry you flight. Security tight. Rebels might blow up planes," the driver added with a wild look.

A mile or so down a barren road they got into another long, unmoving queue. The driver turned off his engine and explained that once they passed a security check they would be put on a bus that would take them to the terminal. "A bus!" Donuts repeated, as if the idea was preposterous, fantastic, unthinkable; yet it was what they had to do.

The line began to move and soon Donuts and Tweety Bird were dragging their luggage into a badly lit storeroom that looked like a scene set for a murder. They hoisted their luggage onto a conveyor belt which was received by more soldiers who went through everything thoroughly before binding them with yellow plastic bands that read 'Security'. The duo climbed onto a crowded bus and after passing two more mysterious check points arrived at the terminal. More check points awaited them; they produced passports, paid a departure tax and, finally, were issued boarding passes.

* * * * * *

In his room at the New Siam guest house in Bangkok, Jamie watched the early morning rain pelt the rooftops. He smelled toast and began to dress. He couldn't find the crease in his pants and decided to get some laundry done. At breakfast he talked with a boy wearing a T-shirt that warned, "Don't eat yellow ice."

Remembering some Thai, Jamie said, "*Pom mai loo* (I don't know)," when the boy asked how long he'd be staying. Jamie asked him about Samui. The boy shook his head and told him that since they had put in an airport it had been overrun. "Now the hippies can return to Goa and start over." He talked brightly about the island of Koh Chang and said he was going there, then home to Sonkla as soon as he saved enough money. He said that he had worked for a year in Hat Yai before coming to Bangkok.

Jamie left a twenty-five baht tip and went off to walk some of the streets he had roamed on his first visit. He passed through the old monastery grounds by children playing, full of smiles; cats; dogs; a bison. It was as though he had never left. He stopped to watch some monks taking down a sheet that had served as the screen for the previous night's movie. Other monks were busy loading folding chairs onto an open truck. Jamie took a photo

Part Two

of one who held a large bouquet and caught his shaved head and inquisitive look just above the white and red flowers. Jamie crossed a busy street and on Khao San Road marveled at a strange, oversized ice cream cart like something out of a carnival or a dream. It was being pedaled by smiling heavy set man.

Jamie checked an address in his notebook and entered an apartment building's front door. It led through an outdoor courtyard to a wide stairway. There were a couple of doped up Thai teenagers nodding on the steps. Next to the doors were plastic buckets of water, rubber sandals. Jamie rapped lightly at number sixteen and was greeted by Eric.

"*Sabi de my cop?*"

"*Sabi, sabi, sabi.*"

They shook hands and sat at a round table covered with a piece of purple Thai silk. They exchanged stories of what had transpired since they had last seen each other in Pattaya. "The red light districts of Thailand are ruined," Eric said. "Instead of a hundred beautiful girls per man the roles are reversed. And it's getting worse." Eric now divided his time between Bangkok and Chaing Rai but said he might be moving on to Cambodia.

It occurred to Jamie that the angles and geometry of Eric's face seemed somewhat altered. And he felt a nudge of caution as they discussed the Sri Lankan affair.

A cute Thai girl appeared from a back room with a tray of tea. Jamie said hello and she smiled bashfully.

"That's Oy."

Eric went into another room and when he came back he had opium pipes and a wad of the stuff. He turned down the lamp and motioned for Jamie to join him on a low cot that was up against a wall covered with pillows.

"Time to relax," Eric said. "This stuff is from the Hmong tribe, a little village just outside of Chaing Rai."

Jamie sucked in the heavy smoke greedily and felt the old glow spreading through him like a magical, reassuring dream of childhood. Oy knelt before him and fixed a new pipe. The next sensation was of dislocation. Jamie took a sip of the jasmine tea and it seemed to take a lifetime. He floated above the city and heard the music of the angels.

EIGHT

The heat of Hawaii, the most isolated archipelago in the world was already evident in the early morning as Roscoe put on a pair of black sunglasses. He was dressed in a white shirt, tan linen slacks and rubber sandals. He looked out the window. The street was overrun with an exotic brew of near naked ladies headed for Waikiki Beach.

Sal Shields sat at the bar in the Waikiki Hana. His hair was disheveled, his eyes glassy and he gestured tiredly to the bartender. Sal wore a spectacle of a Hawaiian shirt: full of purple lizards, yellow flying fish and white and orange flowers that wildly crowded the rest of the space. Sal repeated his order and the bartender shrugged and bent down to pick up a box of vodka fifths. The bartender was already looking forward to his second shot of dope at noon and wondered how much in tips he could make before then.

Roscoe stood in the hotel lobby. He spotted two men across the room giving him stink eye. Then they looked at each other. They seemed like maybe Eastern Europeans. Roscoe stepped quickly into the elevator right before it closed. He got out on a floor with a group that was headed for a Tiki restaurant. The smell of breakfast and the chatter of hungry people crowded the air. He hurried down the walkway, wedging his way through a crowd who were waiting for tables. Roscoe found another elevator and pressed the button for Parking.

Halfway across the outside lot Roscoe's sixth sense told him that he had miscalculated. One of the men that had been eyeing him was waiting. Roscoe looked back and there was the other one, casually standing in the shade with a toothpick in his mouth. Roscoe picked the thug that looked to be just a trace weaker. He ran towards him and the guy went for his waist holster. Roscoe knocked the shot away at the last second. It boomed in the closed quarters and ricocheted off a wall. The guy swung but Roscoe ducked, moved behind him and took the gun. He held it to the thug's head, which made the second bully stop in his tracks. The approaching thug's expression was at first alert then dreamy. Roscoe knew he was playing.

"Hey over there!" someone shouted.

Roscoe gave his captive a good shove and stuck the gun in his pocket. He moved away at the same time a group of inquisitive tourists, mostly men in flowered shirts and crumpled canvas hats, arrived on the scene.

Down a side street Roscoe dashed and after a couple of turns went into a hotel. When he felt for the gun he found it was gone. It seemed to have just disap-

Part Two

peared. From the window in the lobby he saw one of the gunners being pursued by a cop. Just as he was about to step out the other one seemingly out of nowhere appeared and, with that same casualness, took a slow look around.

Roscoe moved back, behind the curtain. He chanced another peek; guy was still there. Roscoe headed back a corridor and left by a side exit. Outside was a gift shop, a Bangoh-bank machine and two elderly women in hideous muumuus and leis talking on pay phones with backs shaped like enormous shells. He stepped up to one of the phones and peeked around the shell. The gunner was gone.

Back in his room, Roscoe's clothes stuck uncomfortably to him and he peeled them off and took a shower. He let the hot then cool water run through his hair numbing his head pleasantly. He called room service for a bottle of rum, some cokes, limes and ice. He would have one or two, he told himself, and put the rest in the mini fridge for later with Nora. Who were the gunners? He didn't know.

Roscoe stayed in the rest of the evening and got slowly toasted and watched TV. In the morning, he was hung over and when he went into the kitchen to make coffee his head exploded like a bare light bulb being smacked with a bat. A flash of fluorescent, yellow light shot through his brain and he fell into a deep black pool of emptiness.

Time had passed. How much? He didn't know. Roscoe heard what he thought was dogs barking in another room before he recognized it as German being shouted. He was on the floor, his hands and feet were tied and numb and he had one hell of a headache. He was in a narrow room with one small window. A curtain allowed only a thin shard of light. Footsteps were approaching.

The thugs from the parking lot came into the room. They wore stupid, vicious grins; one grabbed at his privates and made a face. The other opened his yap and panted and Roscoe felt his fear turn into a kind of sickness and hate.

The panter leaned down and grabbed Roscoe's nose and twisted it till it smarted and Roscoe smelled the grease on his hand. Then someone else was talking: it was the German Roscoe had heard.

The man was somewhere in his forties, deeply tanned with short white hair. He wore a thin mustache and a gray seersucker suit. The man instructed the oafs to untie him. One hissed but, obediently, they did his bidding.

PORTS OF HELL

The gunners almost lovingly massaged life back into Roscoe's limbs, then helped him along behind the white haired man up a staircase. They stopped at a door and the man opened it with a card key.

Inside, the high ceilinged room was filled with palms, flower beds, fountains and deep pools full of koh. Across the room on an elevated marble section, stood an exceptionally beautiful Asian woman. The German went to one knee, bowed, then spoke. The two gunners pushed Roscoe down to his knees and knelt beside him. The floor was covered in a thick coiled hemp. The Asian woman was dressed in a shimmering gown. Her hair was black and blunt cut with bangs. She wore blue lipstick. She had one dead eye.

"This is the man that is here to recover—"

"Why doesn't he speak?" she interrupted.

She looked at Roscoe.

"Speak quickly if you want to live," the German snarled. The elaborate handle of a knife Roscoe had failed to notice earlier stuck out of his wide belt.

"My name is Dan Roscoe. I'm a private investigator and I specialize in tracking down missing persons and missing goods."

Roscoe got the feeling nobody knew what he was talking about as he looked for some acknowledgment. He pressed on.

"This Hawaiian caper was handed to me by Shields, Shields and Shields out of New York." The woman's mouth moved a millimeter. Her one eye brightened slightly. "Sal Shields pulled a fast one on his brothers by snatching a sum of five mil and some ancient, mystical disk. It seems that—"

"The disk is mine," she said.

Roscoe nodded and gestured towards two butterfly chairs on another level between them. She nodded approval, stepped down and took one herself. The German and the two gunners backed up on their knees when she spoke to them tersely in a unknown language. Then she turned to Roscoe.

"I know all about Salvadore Shields. He's is a collector of ancient art, occult books, shrunken heads and such. The disk was stolen thousands of years ago and by mishap and misadventure it has passed through many unfortunate hands. Each person who has kept the disk has met an early demise. Salvadore has so far evaded this due to his practice of certain rituals of my world."

"And what world is that?" Roscoe asked. A thin, enigmatic smile flickered across her lips and her good eye seemed to melt something deep inside of him.

Part Two

"You would not know it—Akar, crossed by a thousand miles of sea from Lemuria."

The room crackled with blue electricity and the two gunners framed in the doorway were transformed before his eyes into lean native guards in loincloths. They held feathered spears. They moved silently and squatted in corresponding corners. The German stepped into the doorway and another transformation took place: he turned into a mulatto. He wore a turban of white and gold, a fancy mustache, a long white shirt that reached to his knees. The woman rose and motioned Roscoe to join her on the lanai. It overlooked Diamond Head and for a moment brought him back to reality. "The money means nothing to me. But the disk belongs in my world."

"What just happened in there?"

"You have fallen into a mystery, Dan Roscoe."

"So I'm to believe you've traveled in time."

"You saw the transformations?"

"Yes... but..."

She leaned forward, looked deep into his eyes and suddenly they were hanging in the sky. Waikiki below them.

"Now?"

"Okay!"

And then they were back on the lanai.

"The disk contains a red mirror belonging to our seer. It is used to communicate with the Visitors."

She studied Roscoe. "You need more proof?"

"No," he said, because he knew it was true. Either that or he had lost his mind. But a deal was still a deal, so he asked how he would be compensated.

"A pouch of diamonds when you deliver the disk," she said.

Roscoe followed a hunch and asked, "But why haven't you retrieved it yourself?"

Her face showed no change of emotion.

"I told you Salvadore has learned a protective ritual. You must be the Transactor. Once the disk is returned Salvadore will come to a very bad end. Nothing can be done about that."

"And me?"

"If you are an honorable Transactor it will not affect you. Betrayal would bring the curse to you."

"I've never betrayed a paying client yet," Roscoe said.

Back on the street Roscoe felt the weird vibe gradually leave but knew he'd never be the same. He decided to spend some time on a barstool in the lounge at the hotel. After his third drink one of the hotel boys capered over and handed him a note from Nora.

PORTS OF HELL

He went up to his room and had a shower. On the table he picked up a half pack of Winstons Nora had left behind. Roscoe hadn't had a cigarette in two years. At first he just smelled the pack; then, as if in a trance, pulled one out and lit it. The smoke rushed through his lungs in a dizzying, poisonous, pleasurable burst. For a moment his head seemed to float high above him. He made himself another drink and put in a call. He got a recorded message. He left a short one.

* * * * * *

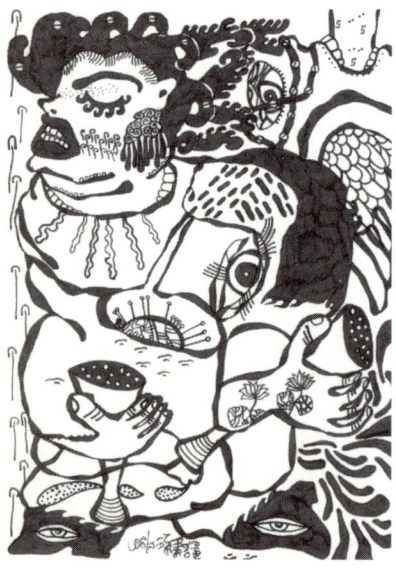

Jamie looked at the blue bay of Puerto Angel, Mexico. A half moon of beach lay on either side. He was listening to a symphony of wild bird songs. He pondered the philosophy of a book he had recently read. He had liked the book yet questioned its basic principle, that one could be in perfect harmony with all life. This was troubling especially since he had decided that Eric had sold out to the other side or was at the least a double agent. He had warned Elias.

And after all there was the Committee and other hostile agents: what Burroughs had called the Shits. He guessed harmony was possible if all the Shits were gone. The first night, Jamie had helped a metallic blue bug out of his cabin rather than kill it and yet was bitten by others during the night. In the morning he had found a ghastly spider under his shirts. He had grabbed a shoe and killed it. Jamie decided to take each incident as it came.

Jamie walked back to his cabin. The giant wasp that buzzed by would not be killed he decided, nor would the nest outside the door be disturbed. He hoped he was making the right decision. Jamie sat for a few minutes and continued to send the thought that he wouldn't bother them, if they didn't bother him.

Jamie looked out over the

Part Two

woods. White butterflies as big as napkins floated down the path. Yellow and blue spotted ones circled a knotty tree. A red butterfly that looked like velvet peeked out of a bush, disappeared. After dark he would continue his study of the paths under a star filled sky. He kicked off his sandals and browsed through a book on the Indians of North America. He knew the pulse of the ocean would surge within him after his first day of swimming. He was glad to be back in Mexico.

Early the following morning Jamie gazed at the blue surrounding hills in the pink early morning sky.

First to find Anna.

He caught a bus which dropped him off on the side of the dusty road and he walked out towards Zipolite beach. The morning heat was leaden. He peeled off his shirt, then kicked off his sandals but stepped back into them. The sand was too hot; it would be cooler by the water but first he wanted to check the open restaurants and hammock areas that were above the beach.

Jamie hiked to the top of a hill and surveyed the surrounding area. At a small inlet a couple of pot-bellied naked white guys wearing sombreros waded in the heavy surf. Sentry-like cacti sat atop the surrounding hills; below stood coconut palms, the trunks painted a yellowish gold. Bright Indian art adorned a whitewashed wall. Pierced, dread locked, tattooed and very stoned hippies slouched over plates of questionable globs of food. Crude irregular wooden fencing blocked off some areas.

Zipolite looked out to Roca Blanca, the great white rock, the blanca due to bird shit. Zipolite, infamous for its undertows and rip tides; only local, loco surfers here. Zipolite, hipster beach of the dead; infamous too for the dozen or so bodies lost each year. A steady roar of waves crashed and rushed ashore.

Jamie took a square, unfinished wood table with matching chair in an open restaurant and dug his feet in the sand. A kid offered him a loosely rolled joint. Jamie said gracias, took some hits and gave it back.

A well seasoned gringo with combed back white hair was filling in a new arrival. The old gringo wore white pants, yellow shirt and a large gold watch. A fat Mexican vendor with his attaché full of silver jewelry sat down and took a break from the morning sun. Hector strolled over in a flowing, orange shirt and rolled up white pants and set a freshly squeezed orange juice in front of Jamie. With his back to the other customers Hector opened his hand and produced a

PORTS OF HELL

folded piece of paper. It floated to the table; Jamie took it and read an address in Spanish.

Anna walked towards the cassetta. Even from the back Jamie knew it was her. She was barefoot, a pair of sneakers, the laces tied together, hung from her shoulder. She was tanned and trim and Jamie admired her shapely legs and buttocks.

"Hello Jamie."

"Hello Anna."

They walked to Playa Panteon hand in hand. Anna had changed to a racy, black bathing suit and a white T-shirt slung across a shoulder. Jamie wore faded red trunks and a soft white T-shirt that Anna loved and kept stroking. He carried a pack with their beach accessories. They spent the rest of the day sunning, swimming and talking lazily. They bought zapote ice cream from out of a wheeled metal cart. Jamie bought a colorful serape and a pair of silver earrings for her. Anna had a funny conversation with a young girl who carried an entire sliced, frosted cake. Finally Anna bought the cake and passed out the pieces to the other beach children. Anna pulled down the top of her suit exposing tan breasts. Jamie kissed her shoulder. She laid on top of him, feeling his erection, and laughed.

"I think its time we go back now, darling."

* * * * * *

Jamie's cabin was at the top of an irregular path, laid with flat rocks, that wound its way up through the woodsy canyon. The place was full of birds, geckos, frogs, iguana, butterflies, spiders and a wide variety of insects and snakes. Jamie learned that the snakes kept their distance and that you had to practically step on them to entail their wrath. Even the Tragasapo, the "one who swallows frogs," minded its own business—as long as you weren't a frog.

Colorful orioles, squawking blue jays, hooting black crows competed for attention. On the roof a family of iguana moved around. Jamie spoke to a sizable black one who stuck out its demonic head. Around him, small doves fluttered and landed. Sleek crows whistled and drank from a copper colored bird bath which had clay birds mounted along the rim. Jamie watched the ants move the soft petals of the bougainvillea. A frog amidst some purplish plants sized up the new resident. A gecko blew out his magnificent red balloon chest, other things obviously on his lizard brain. Jamie cleaned the cabin, unpacked and arranged his things.

Jamie began his regimen and drank garlic and lime juice before

Part Two

going to sleep but still he felt depleted and came down with a cold. He strung a hammock on the porch. Half dozing in it at twilight he conjured up the Mayan god Chac, the rain god also known as "He who urinates" and "He who lights up the sky." Jamie spoke to Huitzilopachtl, the Aztec god of the sun and war. He went into the cabin, followed by a haze of rainbow colors, and laboriously undressed.

Jamie was instructed to not eat for three days and to abstain from sex for nine. He drank down a bottle of lemon grass and cinnamon tea and fell onto the cot where he would spend the next few days, except for trips to the bathroom and to fetch water from the well.

That night it rained with rolling thunder and lightning.

* * * * * *

On the flight back to San Francisco Tweety Bird discovered something unexpected and unexplainable: he could now drink alcohol and, for the most part, maintain his usual personality. No more mister nice guy.

When Donuts saw this, he too took to drink and the two of them put away a dozen beers apiece. In fact, Tweety could hold it better than Donuts, but Donuts would prove to be the one who usually knew when to quit.

On this occasion, though, Donuts was still learning that lesson and, on one attempt to go to the restroom, he slammed into a lady, then the wall, then fell down. They cut them off at that point.

"See what you did, you fat fuck," Tweety snarled.

Donuts pouted and fell back into his seat. Once again a stewardess had had to procure an extension for his seat belt. He fumbled with it until Tweety helped him.

"Now I got to drink goddamn fruit juice or some shit the rest of the flight," Tweety complained as he strapped him in like an oversized child.

"We've got to sober up anyhow," Donuts argued. "We meet with the Chief tomorrow night."

Three days later, after only two beers apiece, they arrived in the heat of the Puerto Escondido airport. Donuts wiped his brow and looked around. Tweety looked around too, locating their luggage and struggling it off the rack.

After Donuts haggled with six taxi drivers for ten minutes, they took one for no less than the original offer. It was a long, up-and-down, hot, dusty ride to Puerto Angel and Donuts, sitting in the back, moaned at every bump. Tweety, on the other hand, enjoyed it and hummed a version of "The Wayward Wind."

"Donuts, look at this beauty. Driver, how do you say beauty? Beautiful?"

"*Bonita, muy bonita.*"

"Boneesta mucho boneiti," he said, sounding more Italian. He saw Donuts frowning and said to the driver, "He doesn't travel well. Know what I mean?"

The driver turned and looked at him with hooded eyes. "No comprende, *sénor*. You in Meh—he—co now."

"Yeah I know we're in Meh—he—co. Jesus."

They checked into a posada in the fishing village of Puerto Angel; Tweety continuing negotiations, working out of a "Speak-Spanish-Easily" booklet, but mostly using body language and a fistful of new peso notes. The posada had a well stocked bar and the barkeep, a friendly local, saw before him the fistful of pesos. He popped two Coronas and Donuts and Tweety Bird made their first new friend. The barkeep's name was Elario; they called him Larry and he accepted it good naturedly.

* * * * * *

Set back from the road to Zipolite in a little A-frame house not yet completed and guarded by three vicious dogs sat an unfamiliar figure at the kitchen table. Under the dim overhead lights Bob Malloy had metamorphosed into a creature known as an IS, or Importer Star. His eyes had changed completely: black and depthless. His skin had turned waxy and yellow. His shoulder blades protruded and leather wings had appeared on his back. Two bats that had been circling the room crashed into the walls and died. An inhuman sound like faulty drainage pipes came forth from his throat. Malloy howled and the walls shook.

* * * * * *

At 8 A.M. Tweety Bird and Donuts, in new sombreros, made their way down to the beach. Donut's shirt featured swordfish, waves, birds, sailboats, guys fishing off them. The duo settled under a palapa at a wooden table. The waiter brought them a menu. "*Buenos dias,*" Tweety intoned to the waiter, who was scrutinizing them. He had already heard about the two barracho gringos known behind the scene as *Sénor* Gordo and *Sénor* Iguana.

"*Buenos dias amigos.* Would you like sum breakfast? Sum nice huervos rancheros. Sum tortillas. Sum fruitas?"

"No. No. *Nada amigo?*"

"*Si.*"

Part Two

"No, later—how you say—later?"

"*Luego.*"

"*Luego* then. What's your name?"

"*Si, luego.*"

"No," Tweety said, exasperated already. He sounded out their names. The waiter tried. "Tweet-tee bid?" Tweety nodded and ordered "dos Coronas." Tweety's beer always foamed at the neck since he had the habit of slamming it down on the table. Today Donuts stated a cautionary warning. "Remember, tomorrow we mustn't drink. Coffee only. We must locate the site."

Tweety gave his mocking, lizard like smile. "*Mánana*, Donuts my man, *mánana.*"

"*Grassias,*" Tweety said to Ecidro, who they called Eddy and who, all smiles, delivered the next round.

NINE

At the Waikiki Hana, Dan Roscoe stepped out of the elevator, went to Sal Shield's door and rang the bell. Sal Shields answered wearing a too small, white, terry bathrobe with the hotel's name spelled across the pocket. The robe was half undone and he looked lit.

"What'dya want?" he asked with a menace Roscoe wasn't expecting. He was unshaven and his eyes were bloodshot and watery.

"I need to talk with you." Roscoe said and stepped in. That surprised Sal and made him mad. He came at Roscoe.

"What d'ya mean?" he slurred, puffing himself up.

Roscoe shot out a short, solid punch straight to the nose. He didn't want to hurt him, just wanted his attention. He wanted him to know it wasn't cool to be an asshole.

"Aw fuck," Sal cried; he held his nose and sat down on a chair. "Maybe ya broke it. What the hell d'ya want anyway?"

"Your brothers sent me to collect the money and the artifact you stole." A wave of panic swept over Sal's face until he managed to calm himself.

"I have nothing to say," he stated, feeling his nose gingerly. Roscoe started to come at him thinking he'd give him a good one two punch and maybe a kick. "Wait a goddamn minute," Sal pleaded. "Okay, okay, I'll tell ya. I lost everything. Every fucking thing."

"I'll need more than that."

"To that fucking bitch. To that brilliant fucking bitch. I'm on the level here." His voice was becoming whiny and desperate. "You're gonna have to find her. I don't know why I did it. I was possessed." He looked at Roscoe with wide eyes. "Don't believe it? Well you'll have to, and it's the truth."

Roscoe gave him his "don't give me that shit" look. "Go ahead, look at that letter there on the desk," Sal whimpered and stared at the floor.

Roscoe picked up the neatly written letter on the hotel's stationery. He read it and yes, Sal explained to his brothers all he had just told him. Roscoe hooked a chair with a toe, turned it around and sat down.

"Sal," he said, "you have some talking to do. Where's the disk? You'll have to tell me much more about this woman."

Sal was eyeing a bottle of scotch longingly so Roscoe got up to fetch the bottle and two glasses. There was no soda or ice left but it was very good scotch. Roscoe handed Sal a drink and he licked his lips and tried some. He took another sip and closed his eyes.

"She has the disk. My life is probably over."

"Tell me about it."

With a resigned look he began, "I was enchanted. I'm sure of it now." He tossed down his drink and looked at Roscoe hopefully. Roscoe poured another. "When I met her I felt something. The air seemed to shimmer as she stood before me. A goddess, I tell you. Well that's what I thought. I was sunk. She seemed to be every actress, model, dancer, woman in the street I had ever lusted for. A sorceress. I was bewitched, bedazzled and all that."

"What happened?"

"What happened was I was a goner. From that moment on I thought of nothing else and through sex, the magical protection I had built up dissolved. She—"

"Her name?" Roscoe interrupted. "Her background?"

Sal looked at him blankly. Sadly he looked around the room as if she had just left and maybe had left something behind, anything. Roscoe had had enough and grabbed him by the bathrobe.

"Awright! Awright!" Sal pulled back flinching. "She has many names, Aicha Qandicha, Lalrona, but in this reincarnation it was Alexis Howard. She's from Honolulu, at least that's what she told me. She worked for an escort service. A whore no less," he said this with a newly found indignation but then his face again turned sad and he looked close to tears. "I didn't care, don't care. I told her I'd be her slave and she just laughed."

"Last address and the name of the agency she worked for."

Dan Roscoe found himself talking like a B movie PI, which he sometimes did just for the fun of it. He fished out his notebook and

Part Two

a stub of a pencil. Sal thought for a minute and gave him the information.

"And the money. In bills?"

"Yes, yes, a black briefcase."

One cliché after another, Roscoe thought. "And the disk?"

"Yes she has it. She's a powerful witch."

Roscoe poured him another drink as well as one for himself. Sal mumbled about his plans to search the South Seas for some protection against the "Curse of the Red Mirror," as he called it.

He checked the phone book there on the table and saw that Sal told the truth. He would ask Nora about the escort service; maybe she even knew her. The Waikiki scene couldn't be too big. Sal suddenly lurched for the Scotch bottle Roscoe had left on the floor.

Roscoe left and took a walk through the tourist filled streets past the ABC stores, souvenir stands, Japanese noodle shops and two Hari Krishna selling books and incense. Someone was selling ball chasing weasels and toy black apes that moved to a loop of the Macarana.

He tried Alexis Howard's number. It was disconnected. He walked through the International Market Place. Torches were lit. Hawaiian music was being played somewhere. Bowls of plastic bananas, guava and pineapples were on pedestals leading the way to a man-made waterfall. At a small restaurant he had an Ahi sandwich and a beer. He walked back to his room. By the entrance, Roscoe saw the two gunners and did a double take. They were in their previous incarnations, dressed in leisure suits and straw hats. Roscoe flipped his cigarette at their feet and one raised his lip a quarter inch.

"Aloha," Roscoe said out the side of his mouth. He still wanted to even things up with them even if they were from another time.

Nora hadn't heard of Alexis Howard but maybe knew her by another name. "You know that sounds a lot like Leslie Pernell," she said, adjusting the shower nozzle. Roscoe said he needed a picture of her and that Sal claimed to have none. Nora said she had one of Leslie at her place.

The following day Roscoe arrived at Honey Escort Downtown, HED. It was an off yellow building with a stucco roof. Weeping, Sal had confirmed: Alexis Howard and Leslie Pernell were one and the same.

"Yes?" the attractive receptionist asked with a hint of accusation and flirt. She was an Island girl and her high points were perfect white teeth, dark flashing eyes and a firm bust line. Roscoe told her he needed an escort that had known Leslie Pernell. A lean, too tan, older woman with short white hair and green cat eyes stepped out of a back room and introduced herself as the manager, Carol. She held a long thin cigarette, took his card and escorted him to a back office that was stuffed with file cabinets and pots of elephant eared plants. A slightly crooked framed photograph above her desk featured Carol riding a surfboard with a sort of crazed look in her eyes.

"I know very little about Leslie. And I didn't know she had an alias. Alexis, eh? She worked for us exactly two weeks." Carol brought it up on a computer screen. "Left with no notice. Had only a couple of dates. Nothing out of the ordinary. Left no forwarding address."

"Did she have any friends here?"

Carol took a long drag and blew out a stream of blue smoke. "Liani. They worked together and Liana brought her into the agency. They knew each other outside of work." Carol looked at Roscoe curiously, "I'd have to charge you the usual fee to see her."

That evening Roscoe went to meet Liani at a bar in Chinatown. He walked by some abandoned brick buildings, cheap bars, a stand selling shaved ice, another Spam sandwiches and another leis and bikini wraps. Roscoe felt a fondness for the down-on-its-heels dilapidated ambiance Chinatown had managed to hold onto. Someone was shooting a film and the block he was headed for was full of trailers and camera crews that commandeered the sidewalk. Tourists and locals stood in clustered crowds, watching. Roscoe worked his way into the Bamboo Lounge and found a table against a wall. He spotted her from her photo and caught her eye. Liani was Filipino, pretty and wore a little black dress. Roscoe ordered drinks and Liani with just a shade of coyness asked why he had requested her. He said he was a private investigator trying to track down stolen money and an ancient artifact.

"Yeah? Somebody I dated?"

She looked at the photograph of "Alexis" and one of Sal Shields. "That's Leslie and her ex. I remember right before she met him, she cut her hair and went blonde."

Was there anyone else involved in this? Roscoe's intuition told him yes, of course. He touched Liani's hand as she sipped her Passion fruit Chablis. "Tell me what you know," Roscoe said.

"Well, she met him on the beach one night. She said it was like destiny, kismet. She felt

Part Two

drawn to him. Said she had never approached a man like that before. She quit then and they went off visiting all the islands. He was a rich businessman, divorced. I saw them together a few times. They looked happy. They were planning marriage and a honeymoon to China."

Roscoe and Liani didn't say anything for a while, just sipped their drinks. She gave him some cozy looks and patted his leg. Two men in suits had entered the bar. They took a table across the room. Cops, Roscoe thought, and Liani acknowledged.

"They bust the street dealers and play games with the working girls," Liani whispered. "We figure they jerk each other off." The two didn't pay them any attention. They huddled into some emotionally charged conversation of their own.

Liani moved her hand further up Roscoe's leg. He noticed her clean nails, neatly manicured, sans polish. She held his arm. Her eyes were all smiles.

"So what's next?"

"Tell me some more."

"Well, they were in love and everything was groovy. One night I was home, alone, dancing, in the buff," she laughed. "And I kept hearing some noise. Then I realized it was someone buzzing. I knew it was her, somehow. She was crying and her makeup was running down her face. I held her and she just cried for a long time. She told me what I suspected. Mister Wonderful was going back to his wife. She'd found them in the sack. But later, after a couple drinks and a joint, she got a whole different attitude. She got a cold look in those beautiful eyes and said, 'You know, fuck him. I'm going to L.A. where I always wanted to go. I'll be just fucking fine.' I told her she could stay with me but when I came home the next night she was gone. She left a note saying thanks and that she'd be in touch. I haven't heard from her. That was a couple of weeks ago."

"Did you see her leave on the plane?"

"Well no, but she must've left the island?"

Roscoe shrugged.

"You don't think anything bad has happened?" Liani asked darkly.

"I don't know much of anything yet."

"Listen, are we going out tonight?"

"Well, I'd like to see your apartment."

They left the bar that had gotten stuffy with other people and smoke. Outside, a tropical drizzle had started and Liani took off her shoes and walked barefoot. She latched onto his arm and they strolled like so many other lovers. Roscoe was looking forward to knowing her better. She said Hawaii was like living in a tiki theme park.

They stopped at a modern apartment building of hive like units that rose into the Honolulu night. The lobby was barren of any personality. The streaked glass needed cleaning. There was some junk mail on a rusty metal bench and burns and spots on the gray indoor outdoor carpet. Liani checked her mailbox out of habit. The elevator was bathed in an otherworldly green light and clanked and groaned as it carried them to her floor. The corridor it stopped on was as blank as any he'd ever seen. A combination of smells that suggested food, medicines and cleaning products haunted the corridors.

Liani's apartment was sparsely furnished on hardwood floors. A white futon in the bed position sat in the middle of the room. A zebra skin hung on a wall near a home entertainment and bar area. Roscoe discovered that Liani was a talented and lovable girl. The sex was nearly telepathic. He spent the night and dreamt he was on a beach surrounded by talking tikis that spoke the queen's strange language. Under a lava influenced sunset, a silent lime green canoe floated by.

* * * * * *

The General was sitting alone in his chamber. He looked at his luminous watch and the eye within a square tattooed on his wrist. "How far does this go?" he said aloud.

There was an ominous shift in the atmosphere—an unnerving undercurrent followed by a melodious voice that drifted through the chamber.

"Until we are in every microcosm of belief and code."

"The Committee are on this," the General offered, with a twinge of weakness he tried unsuccessfully to hide. "The agents are all content slaves," he added with more confidence.

The melodious voice picked up volume and grew edgier. "And Elias and his pack? The resistance? They live!" The voice had become affronting and full of static. The General was visibly shaken. He lowered his head, knowing his existence was on the line, and waited in terror but nothing happened. In a soft voice he asked,

"I continue the operation?"

"Yes, you continue," the voice hissed. "But consult the time table. By the first moon of the next month."

The voice was gone and gradually the General began to relax. Then an urge for sex came over

Part Two

him. The General headed for the hallway where the sex pets were kept. He picked a favorite door and, an hour later, reemerged with his trousers on inside out and a smile plastered on his face.

* * * * * *

Mexico City. Elias and Winks were having breakfast at a restaurant high above the zocalo. The sun was rising above the skyline and the square was coming to life below. In the poisonous air, vendors were setting up stands to sell lottery tickets, sunglasses, Bonsai trees, amber jewelry, giant stuffed rabbits, fake perfumed roses, chewing gum and dolls with black faces. In a boarded up doorway stood a long-haired young man whose face was painted black on one side and white on the other. Strapped to his arms were enormous wooden wings which rested on the sidewalk before him. This Icarus looked down at his wings with a melancholy expression. An occasional passerby dropped a centavo or two into his bowl.

Elias had grown a different kind of mustache; something like Gurdjeiff's. Winks looked exactly the same and was now a functioning transmitter between Elias and the emissaries. Elias reported through him as Winks' eyes rolled back behind his dark Ray Bans.

Winks reported the activity of an occult Yogini in Alaska; a brilliant architect in London and a hypersonic jazz musician in New York who was attaining some prominence: all agents. The latest placement was a guide in Trivanprum India: Loualun Beach, to be exact.

Elias spoke of Jamie Coates and the current affairs in Puerto Angel. Winks asked in an odd high voice; "Malloy? The IS?"

"Yes. Our man is there—with backup."

"Operation Red Mirror."

"Yes. Operation Sun Ray."

* * * * * *

Jamie listened to the breeze move through the trees. He was guided by the moonlight and the stars as he traveled from path to path. The inner red light directed him while he ran and climbed. His breath remained steady. He came to a clearing that overlooked the sea.

The emissary seemed to stir inside his cloak. "The disk installed," he said. "Importer Star."

* * * * * *

Alone in a office, Jamie was waiting for the Mexican Capitan who entered wearing a dark blue uniform. The Capitan sat at his desk and requested and then studied Jamie's passport. Without looking up he asked, "*Sénor* Kuhns, why did you come to Puerto Angel?" Jamie stared at a spot on his forehead directly between his eyes.

"Because I love the coast of Oaxaca very much. I want to bask in the sun, swim in your beautiful bay, and to partake of the local cuisine."

Jamie's gaze moved to a framed picture of the Capitan twenty years younger and 20 lb lighter and still frowning. On a table below the picture stood a few old books, an overturned cloudy glass, a canteen, a walkie talkie and a gleaming, recently cleaned oyster shell ashtray.

"And I need a rest from my work."

"Which is what?" the Capitan asked, looking Jamie in the eye.

"I work with people whot are being released from the prison system. I update their files, make referrals, arrange for their temporary assistance."

"You work for the government?"

"Well, no, it's regulated and monitored by the government, but actually run by a private agency."

"Private police then?"

"No, not really," Jamie didn't feel like elaborating unless he had to.

The Capitan's expression of confusion changed to disapproval as he tapped his bottom front teeth with a pen. His face went blank again but then he reconsidered the passport and handed it back.

"Enjoy your vacation, *Sénor* Kuhns."

When Jamie left the compound he sat on a low wall by some dusty, faded palm trees. In the sand, overturned boats in advanced stages of disrepair surrounded him like the discarded shells of some forgotten race. A smell of sewage lingered, disappeared, came back, riding the breezes from the bay. There was no mistaking the smell of human waste. The "Honey Dippers" must be working, he laughed at the name given to the sanitation team. Behind him were some ramshackle houses, Mexican music coming from a radio in one. A diver walked by wearing only the legs of a wet suit and carrying a spear in one hand, a handful of octopus in the other. On the compound's roof was a satellite dish and the tricolor flag of Mexico. Three navy men in dark blue uniforms, bill hats and combat boots with machine-guns slung over shoulders took a cigarette break at a back door.

* * * * * *

Part Two

Alexis Howard, aka Leslie Pernell, had not left Hawaii according to Izzy the hacker. Roscoe learned something else about her. She was a gym fanatic. He drove out to Work Out Waikiki, WOW!, where Leslie had trained and briefly filled in as an instructor. There was a hippie wearing wire rims behind the reception desk reading a thick, well thumbed book on Eastern philosophy and religion. Roscoe tossed down Leslie's picture.

"Where is she?" he said bluntly.

"Do I know you?" the receptionist asked, narrowing his eyes.

"Well, you better," Roscoe shot back.

The receptionist looked down at his book as if to find the answer there. Two fit, healthy girls in white shorts, tank tops, sneakers and socks sprinted by. A muscular guy from the gym appeared with a name tag that read Tom Roberts.

"Roberts," Roscoe said, "who is this piece of shit we have behind the desk?"

"Er, Evan Collins." Collins looked up, a troubled question moving about his face.

"Okay Collins, you're history. Get your stuff and get out," Roscoe said in his most badass voice.

Collins looked at Roberts, to Roscoe then back to Roberts.

"You're fired, asshole. Beat it. Off the premises before I throw you off."

Collin's mouth had dropped and he wanted to say something, but he couldn't put the words together. The principles of balance that he had just been reading about seemed as though they had never existed.

"In five minutes I'll consider you a trespasser," Roscoe said with his sternest look. Collins hung his head, got up and lumbered off. Roscoe sat on the desk and handed the photo to Tim Roberts.

"Leslie," he said, "and, I'm sorry sir, but who are you?"

"Gordon," Roscoe said giving him a bogus card and his hand a quick vigorous shake. "Previously the legal end, but as of yesterday fifty percent owner of WOW!"

Roberts was impressed.

"Tell me about Leslie. This is a private matter," Roscoe winked.

"Tell me whatever you know." Roberts looked at the photo. "Well, she was one of the girls in line to come on full time, but Honey Escort Downtown offered her more money. And the report we got back through the owners, well—you and company, was that the salaries were fixed for the year."

"Ridiculous," Roscoe said. Roberts looked at him then

back at the photo as though it had spoken to him. "She was seeing Shiro's driver. Shiro owns the escort service." Roberts was thinking that perhaps he could rise within the organization, having met an owner. "The driver's name is Emanuel Moray, he's from the Philippines and known as Manny. He's well known. A professional kick boxer. He was once the bodyguard for the middleweight Lopez but was fired for paralyzing an overzealous fan. He was indicted and served two years in Helawa. Mister Gordon—" Roberts seemed to boost himself up a notch and Roscoe could see he was ready to lay on some spiel.

"Yes Tom?"

"Well Mister Gordon, I've been with Work Out Waikiki for two years and have been instrumental in a few, er, key situations."

"Yes, we have our eyes on you."

A door opened somewhere, letting out the sound of energetic voices and bodies hitting mats, then shut again.

"Well I've heard the rumor that Richard Madison is returning to the Mainland."

"And you think you can fill his shoes?"

"This whole past month that's exactly what I've been doing. Sir, I—" Roscoe cut him off wanting to get on his way, having gotten the information he was looking for.

"Keep it under your lid, Tom, and the job is yours," Roscoe said to his beaming face. "You'll be notified." Roberts showed Roscoe Leslie Pernell's personal file.

On the way out Roscoe had to chuckle, especially over the guy he'd fired. It had been his experience that if he could convince himself that he was somebody else, others would easily believe him. He fancied that he could have followed an acting career had the cards been dealt somehow differently.

So Leslie went with Manny, the driver for Shiro, the owner of Honey Escort Downtown. Roberts had told him where Shiro's house was located, in the prestigious Haiku Garden area which overlooked the Valley of the Temples. He drove out there.

A black Lincoln pulled up from around the back of Shiro's impressive house and parked near the entrance. Manny looking like a small ape, was at the wheel. Another man with a big bald head towering over shoulders like Cadillac bumpers and Shiro, a small Japanese man, came out and climbed in the back of the car. All three showed as much variance in emotion as you'd expect from three macadamia nuts. It was early evening as Roscoe tailed the Lincoln to the entrance

Part Two

of a fancy Italian restaurant. Shiro and Baldy got out.

So Manny was not at the level to dine with his higher ups? Must bug him.

The maitre d' did a combination greeting, bowing and directing gestures for Shiro. Nice place. Sawdust on the hardwood floors, tanned college kids delivering the food and drinks. The fare looked and smelled good. Roscoe decided to eat as well.

He took a table near the bar, where Shiro couldn't leave without Roscoe seeing him. He ordered a mushroom pasta deal, glass of Claret and a side salad. When he was finished he went outside for a smoke. Roscoe watched Shiro and Baldy coming out, Baldy lighting his boss's fat Robusto with a lighter like a small blow torch.

Roscoe followed the Lincoln to the Marina and watched them go aboard a yacht. An hour passed and he was just about to get out and relieve himself when they came back out. He tailed them back to Shiro's place. Manny put the car away and reappeared in his own red Datsun.

In Pearl City, the Datsun finally pulled into a parking space. Manny got out and entered a nine story apartment complex. A vine was beginning to work its way up one side and was approaching the third floor. Roscoe took a near frantic piss in some bushes.

Roscoe watched the building hoping to see a light come on but none did. He wondered if Manny was in one of the other units in the back.

The moon was waning and there was a coolness in the air; then he saw Manny's profile at one of the windows.

Roscoe figured they were waiting for any heat to blow over before flying out.

His job was two-fold. First was to locate Sal Shields which he had. He had relayed that information to Sonny Shields who had expressed displeasure that his wayward sibling had naught. Roscoe had tried to reassure him that he'd retrieve everything. "Why not act confident?" was his motto. And he was now looking at the place where he figured the stash was. Leslie, he'd bet, had another dye job and hardly ever went out. A different hair style and big dark glasses. Runs out once in a while for snacks, booze and smokes.

There was a store, a bar and a newsstand down the street. Roscoe walked to the bar, went in and ordered a coffee from the red headed, red faced bartender. It was another upscale place, waiters with ties and long white aprons serving hors d'oeuvres to the well heeled customers. He bought a couple bags of macadamia nuts. They seemed to sell them everywhere. At the store he bought some gum, a macadamia nut chocolate bar, cigarettes and a newspaper. Back in the car he read, snacked and smoked. Later he put the seat back and caught a few winks. At dawn Roscoe sprinted over to the gas station and used the rest room. He washed his face and popped the last of the gum in his mouth. On the way back to the rental car he almost stopped dead in his tracks. Manny was coming out of the building twirling his car keys. Roscoe forced himself to continue to walk causally. Manny only glanced at him and headed to his car.

Two hours crawled by.

The morning was heating up. Roscoe felt certain Leslie would make an appearance soon and he was right. Sun dress, kerchief on her head, back to brunette, enormous dark glasses, shopping bag type pocketbook. She looked up and down the street. An old timer in a Panama suit came out of the place next door, glanced at her and walked on. A kid wearing puka shells screamed, chasing another kid on a red bike. Before she turned the corner, Roscoe was in the building double checking the directory.

At the door, he jammed in the wedge, once, twice and popped it.

The room held a beige couch, a coffee table overflowing with magazines, ashtrays, empty glasses, pizza crust. A small TV and boom box sat in a corner. The kitchen and bathroom were messy too. The bedroom held an unmade double bed, rattan chest of drawers, some open, overstuffed and a sliding door closet. He figured to start there. Although sun filtered into the room, intuition told him to try the overhead light. He did and nothing happened. He looked at the square covering and there was just something off. Roscoe stood on a chair and with his Swiss Army knife undid the screws. With just one side down he knew he had it. The long bulbs had been removed and there was a piece of dark material and there, in neat rows, was the cash. He laid it all on the bed, looked around for a bag and found a backpack in the closet behind about thirty pairs of Leslie's shoes. Leslie, it appeared, had already done some shopping.

"Drop it and turn around slowly."

It was Leslie; Roscoe turned and found her steadily holding a black automatic aimed at his head.

"Did you really think you could just waltz in here and—on the floor now!" He began to obey but could see she was struggling

Part Two

with what to do next. The phone rang. Acting on the distraction, he tackled her. She hit him sharply in the head with the gun butt. It stunned him but he got on top and took it away. She continued to squirm and curse and thrash around; getting an arm free she grabbed his testicles. He punched her square in her pretty face. She lay still after that. The phone stopped ringing. Roscoe doubled over and suffered a pain and nausea that only a man can know. When Leslie came around he wasted no time, grabbing her to give her a couple of vicious shakes. She looked at him, glassy eyed. Roscoe stuck the gun in her nose. In the mouth, he thought, was just a cliché.

She trembled.

"The disk?"

"The Troll. The friggin' Troll!"

The Troll doll was next to a stack of fashion magazines. Behind the day glo purple hula grass skirt taped to the belly was a silver disk a bit larger than a silver dollar. "Like a miniature flying saucer," Roscoe thought looking more at the Troll's frightful matching hair and insane face. He pocketed the disk and filled the backpack. Leslie was crying softly when he left.

Roscoe started up the Mazda Mystic. Before he had gone on this little romp he had had the foresight to relocate to a hotel out by the airport and now he would get a different rental.

The money was Shields, Shields and Shields but the disk? Did that indeed belong to the queen from another time? Undecided on what to do, he decided to do nothing for a while.

Roscoe had a shower and a cold beer at the new hotel. He went for a swim in the lotus shaped pool, ordered room service and watched TV. After an Elvis in Hawaii special was a talk show that featured Honolulu residents. Two old timers he particularly liked wore tilted back sailor caps, island print shirts and talked about a Honolulu of the past. They described a steamy port full of seafaring men, rowdy bars and tattoo parlors. They showed pictures of themselves in front of a tiki bar looking like a couple of sea savvy cads. Roscoe learned that the aloha shirt had evolved from the 1930s Waikiki beach boy scene. Outside the window, gentle palms swayed and somewhere a wooden percussion instrument tapped out a haunting tattoo. Then a jet took off. Dan Roscoe slept soundly. The little black automatic under his pillow.

In the morning, Roscoe took a walk on the airport road lined with palms that led eventually to some misty mountains. He

PORTS OF HELL

stopped walking when he saw Manny's red Datsun pull into a lot. Manny and Leslie got out and walked over to a terminal. Manny talked to a ticket agent whom he appeared to know. The agent referred to a computer but shook his head when he looked back at Manny. Manny frowned and Leslie pouted. Her lips looked puffy. Roscoe hid behind a Honolulu Advertiser.

The front page story stunned him: the torture death of vacationing businessman Salvadore S. Shields of New York's Shields, Shields and Shields. Sal was found in his hotel room tied to a chair and gagged, missing his right thumb and right ear. He had been stabbed and burned repeatedly. Police were investigating.

Roscoe figured it was Manny's work. They now have my name, he thought coldly, and also knew that he hadn't flown out. Manny and Leslie walked back to the car and retrieved overnight bags from the trunk. Roscoe watched them walk next door and go into the hotel where he was staying. They were camping, waiting for their reader to tag his flight and notify them. Roscoe had registered with his second ID knowing never to be anyone for too long. He checked out over the phone, went out a side entrance and drove back into the city. He wanted to know more about the queen and the gunners. He found a room on Hotel Street, not far from Chinatown.

At a pay phone he called the airport hotel and asked for Mister Emanuel Moray. They put him through.

"Hello?"

"Manny old buddy."

"Who's this?"

"This is the dude you're looking for dumb fuck."

Silence.

"Oh Manny boy," Roscoe cooed. "Isn't Shiro wondering where you are?"

Silence

"Hey I'm talking to you babe."

In a weird demonic voice Manny said, "You haven't gotten away yet.

"You'll never know when I'll be at your back."

"It doesn't appear you're that bright," Roscoe said. "Let me run it down to you. I called you. I'm the one holding. Remember, the money, the artifact? You there, Manny boy?"

"I've got ears and eyes everywhere," Manny persisted, his voice growing even darker. "This is the island. I'll find you."

Roscoe shook off a slight chill and said, "Don't you think Hawaii Five-O is gonna want to talk with you?" He wasn't prepared for Manny's answer.

"We've already been cleared,"

Part Two

Manny laughed. "But I'm sure they'll want to chat with the visiting PI pig from Miami. And don't think I don't own some choir boys. There's nowhere to run, Roscoe."

"Let's check off a few things here," Roscoe said trying to gain back ground. "One, I have the loot. Two, I have the artifact."

"Fuck you," Manny spat and hung up.

In the cramped phone booth Roscoe thought about what to do next. He put in a call to the most connected operations man he knew. Richard Lansing, out of Chicago. He got his message machine and began to speak when Lansing cut in.

"Roscoe old boy. What'ya up to?"

"Lansing, hey I'm in Honolulu. I need someone friendly to talk with at Hawaii Five-O."

"How about McGarrett?" Lansing laughed. "You son of a bitch, in Hawaii and I'm stuck in this blizzard."

"Give me a name."

"Oh lets see—Stevenson. Good guy. Worked with me here once, Mafioso porn thing. He's all right. Airtight."

"Is that Sergeant or what?"

"Detective."

"Thanks."

* * * * * *

"Detective Stevenson here," a young voice said. Roscoe introduced himself, his referral and gave him an edited version of the case.

"Don't worry 'bout a thing Roscoe. Moray's right though, there's no way he could've done it. He was playing in a golf tournament on Maui. Tell me more about the Asian lady and her cohorts." Roscoe told him but skipped the fantastic parts thinking he would find him a lunatic. Roscoe described the queen as an eccentric collector. The detective gave him a private number and told him to check with him periodically.

That night, dressed in a newly laundered set of whites, Roscoe took a long walk on the beach. He thought about Sal and his unfortunate meeting with Leslie Pernell aka Alexis Howard. Roscoe entered the lobby of the Queen Kapiolana. He took the elevator to the other queen's floor but, on instinct, took it back down to the busy lobby. He spotted one of the gunners approach the front desk. The clerk handed him some mail and the ape stuffed it into his jacket pocket. One envelope stuck out invitingly. Merging into a crowd just as the gunner entered the elevator Roscoe snatched the envelope. Addressed to HED Inc., in Lanikai, it was a voucher for "items received," by

PORTS OF HELL

"IS" in Chicago.

It was another glorious day as Roscoe drove along a patchwork of taro fields by an enchanted shoreline, listening to Hawaiian slack key guitar on the radio. He traveled a curved boulevard lined with banyan trees by hotels that looked like fantasy palaces. He lit a cigarette and almost forgot why he had set out.

At the hotel, a jumpy man in the lobby had tried to interest him in a day trip to the Polynesian Village, a goat luau, or a sunset catamaran ride; Roscoe told him he had plans but absently took some of the glossy brochures. They lay there on the seat. Roscoe turned off the AC and shot down the windows.

TEN

Donuts and Tweety Bird were sitting at a wooden table on the beach, under a red-and-white striped beach umbrella. Tweety slouched in a wooden chair while Donuts more than filled a large white plastic one. They wore bright, touristy T-shirts with scenes and adverts decorating the fronts. Donuts' advertised Huatulco with birds, boats, anchors and seaman's knots. Tweety's Puerto Escondido shirt featured an orange sun and a surfer riding the Mexican pipeline.

It was 7:13 A.M. and they were just tasting their first Coronas. An accompanying new passion for the duo was smoking. Previously, Tweety had smoked lightly and Donuts not at all. Now they both smoked almost continuously, Marlboro or the Mexican imitation Montana, an open carton of which lay between them on the table.

"Tweety, I think it's time we locate that cafe."

"Business, business, business—is that all you think about?"

Donuts cocked an eye.

"Listen, the Committee is not something to fuck with. We were just plain lucky in Sri Lanka. That could have been the end of the game. We've got another shot here and it seems simple enough. Keep an eye on the place, mark the activity; talk with the owner a bit and wait for somebody to pick up the reports."

"Sounds fuckin' boring," Tweety muttered. "I just wanna sit here and look at the water." The landscape around them dripped with color. The bay so blue it seemed unreal, more like Technicolor. "We deserve some R' n R." Tweety said and looked over at Ecidro. "My friend here talks too *mucho*? *Mas*?" Ecidro thought he might want more beer

Part Two

and pointed to the half empty bottles. "*Mas?*"

Donuts stared at their bottles for a moment and said, "Yes. Si, Eddy, dos mas."

Tweety smiled, "Now you're talking, Donuts my man." He lit another Montana with his plastic lighter that advertised Huatulco.

* * * * * *

Bob Malloy was crabbing his way over to the bar at the posada. His head, moving on turrets, slowly surveyed the room. There was a caged parrot near the bar who let out a screech when it saw him. He gave the bird an otherworldly look and it fell silent. Then the bird let out a wolf whistle, asked "Como esta?" and finally just made some low cooing sounds. Elario said buenos tardes to Malloy, got no response so asked in English what he wanted to drink. Malloy fell into his friendly human mode and said, "Oh, sorry *sénor*, my mind was elsewhere. Let me have a slug of mescal."

"*Si*," Elario smiled. "*Mas forte. Mas bueno.*"

He dragged up the big bottle with colorless nanches on the bottom. He opened it and gave Malloy a sniff.

"Whee—that there is some sauce. Hello."

The mescal was served in small glazed cups. Malloy tossed the first two straight down after a lick of lime and salt.

"Now give me one to sip, amigo."

"*Mas?*"

"*Si, mas.*"

Elario waited to watch him toss that one too but instead he took a dainty sip and smiled.

"*Dispacio, dispacio.*"

"*Si.*"

Elario moved away to fill another order that required him to use the electric ice shaver. Malloy had registered everyone in the bar. There were no agents nor the decoys. He let himself relax but continued to scan the people on the street that passed by: tourists, folks from Oaxaca City, Mexico City, backpackers from Europe and the States and a few street vendors. Two men were stroking their prize-fighting cocks; uniformed school children, sailors walked by but nothing was out of place. Tonight Malloy would complete the process with the Capitan. It had been almost too easy to possess him. Tonight, though, his tongue and entrails would turn to rubber and he could install the disk. Malloy sipped the mescal and considered the report he had received regarding an agent in the area and the arrival of the two decoys. He would watch the decoys. See who watched them.

When Elario got another break Malloy grabbed his attention.

"Amigo."

Their eyes locked and Malloy latched onto his neocortex. A moment passed where Elario looked like he was in a trance as he wiped an imaginary spot on the bar top. Malloy leaned forward, studying him and listening to what he had to tell.

At midnight, Malloy again took his chair at his kitchen table. The metamorphosis was quicker. A crop of white fuzzy hair grew out of his head and chest and his eyes went all poppy like a frog. His howl made the dogs run off and hide behind a wood pile. His flesh turned waxy and his shoulder blades rose dramatically as though he was suddenly hoisted up on hooks. He rocked to and fro, then stood as still as a frozen mime. A double of Malloy with leathery wings disengaged, ascended through the ceiling and moved silently across the night sky. Fantastic birds that only traveled under the stars veered off in each direction when they sensed the presence. The moon was a cup of luminous potion, a magical remnant from the beginning. Below was the bay of Puerto Angel.

Capitan Gomez inspected the toilet, annoyed when he found a splatter of urine from the last occupant on the seat. Had he caught the culprit, he would have had him clean all the bathrooms for a month under his own strict inspection. Give him a pumice stick and have him get every bit of yellow, crystallized encrustation that had built up. The Capitan considered the possibility that the Admiral was the culprit, but he dismissed that. The Admiral, after all, mostly used his private bath which boasted the only tub on the base and which was the brunt of a joke: "the Admiral needed the bathtub to 'float his ducky'." One of Gomez's spies had shared this mindless joke.

Gomez cleaned the seat and tossed the toilet paper into the plastic bag that lined the wicker basket. He padded back to his room with a flashlight in his hand in case something warranted an investigation.

When he laid down on his cot his limbs went limp. His head seemed fastened to the pillow, then he was tossed over on his back. A prehistoric figure of Malloy with erect phallus and a mouth that stretched and contorted like something out of Bosch floated into the room and hovered above him. The IS ejaculated, screeched and stuck the disk into Gomez's open mouth.

In the morning an enthusiastic Capitan Gomez spoke to three of his men. "I've had the pleas-

Part Two

ure to meet our newest resident, Mister Robert Malloy, a retiree with a celebrated background in the armed services of the United States Marines. As a courtesy, I want you to install a phone at his residence." He handed a paper sack over to one of the men. "And give him these tamales as a token of friendship." One of the men eyed another, then purposely looked away at a fly that had landed on a pastry dish. Gomez spotted a tiny spot on one of the men's white T-shirts which showed above their dark blue shirts. He instructed them all to change their caps for helmets and pointed out the spot to an embarrassed man named Raoul.

* * * * * *

Jamie scooped up some sawdust and dumped it down the compost closet. With a hand broom he swept the few chips that remained on the seat. As the proprietor's note said on the inside door: "Your shit will help the forest grow."

Jamie had pushed himself the previous day to visit the shaman woman who lived about a mile down the road. He had arrived sweaty, dusty and feeling like his blood had turned to lead. In a dim area behind a screen she had him lay on a cot. Once his breathing had quieted, she had approached with a mask that was a replica of Elias' face.

"This is the present for you," the shaman woman had said, holding it above him and chanting something in Zapoteca. "I will place it now on your face."

The mask had smelled of lavender and had felt cool. A fluting sound had entered the room and a vibration had ensued and spread throughout his body. Sometime later, the mask had been removed.

The red glow had been recharged. Jamie had also experienced an intense sharpening of his vision and senses. He had thanked the shaman woman and had paid the small amount she had asked for.

"It was my duty, *Sénor* Coates."

COMMITTEE VIOLENCE WASHINGTON. D. C.

A protest in front of Committee headquarters turned violent when demonstrators broke into the building smashing windows with rocks and sticks. Others tried to rush the entrances but guards successfully held them back. Six demonstrators were taken to the hospital with minor to serious injuries.

Trisha Ladd, spokeswoman for the demonstrators, told the press that, "The Committee is controlled by malevolent, life threatening entities that have infiltrated the police force and the armed services." The English born writer cited supposed past exploits by Committee agents to wage warfare against any opposition. A few fringe writers have sided with Ladd.

The Committee Chief spoke briefly to reporters and stated the agency's objective: "A long-term comprehensive study and intervention of our men and women of the law enforcement and the armed service." He cited cases and statistics which pointed to the Committee's success with specific arrests and an overall increase in morale.

* * * * * *

The beach vendor sat his case of silver rings, earrings and necklaces in front of Tweety Bird, who was on his sixth Corona. In a matter of minutes Tweety bought three silver rings, placing all of them on his right hand. The vendor tried to interest this crazy gringo who didn't even try to barter into buying a necklace too, but Tweety waved him away with "*Mánana, mánana.*"

The vendor smiled. "Don't forget me. My name is Elvis."

"Elvis," Tweety laughed, "that'll be hard to forget."

Donuts looked at Tweety with amusement that turned to disapproval.

"After this beer I'm following the map with or without you," he said.

Tweety mockingly repeated what Donuts said before adding, "Shut up already. Did I say I wasn't coming?"

Donuts slapped down some pesos, put a pack of Marlboro in his pocket, drank the last from his bottle and stood. Tweety, who had been ready to order another, frowned and watched Donuts turn and amble off down the beach. Ecidro appeared at the table and Tweety pushed the open carton of smokes towards him. "Eddy, keep these for us." Ecidro understood what Tweety had said more through the gesture and nodded.

"*Si, Sénor* Tweet-ee."

"Yeah, *Buenos* fucking *dias*," Tweety muttered and headed off after Donuts.

An hour later found Donuts and Tweety Bird standing under a tree, waiting for the shade to cool them, which it never really did. Donuts moped his brow and neck with a handkerchief. He glared at the map before him and cursed.

"What fucking dirt road? There's dirt roads everywhere."

Part Two

Tweety jabbed at the map. "By the *Huanacaxtle* tree, it says."

"And do you know what a fucking whoanacastle tree looks like?" Donuts bellowed.

"No, but I'll bet this kid does." Tweety nodded towards a boy who was coming up the rough ravine barefoot, effortlessly, carrying a plastic bucket on his head.

"Who an tree?" Donuts said to the boy who looked at him as though he had just landed from Saturn. "Who an" — Tweety dug out his Spanish book — "*Arbol*," he said and pointed to a tree. "*Grande... Huanacaxtle arbol.*"

Donuts produced a five peso coin and gestured to the tree they were under. The kid sat his bucket down and shook his head and his index finger which reminded Donuts of the crazy Sri Lankan head nod. "No no no," the boy said assuming the role of a teacher now giving his dull students a lesson. He pointed up the eroded, rocky, dirt road. "*Huanacaxtle arbol ahi*," the boy said. There stood an enormous tree. Donuts flipped the coin into the air and the kid caught it expertly and stuck it into his pocket. "*Empanada, pina platanos?*" he asked and Tweety said "No *grassias*." The boy picked up his bucket and was halfway up the hill before Donuts and Tweety had taken step one.

They trudged up to the tree and just beyond found an outside cafe with a dirt patio where a rooster and a hen strutted about. The place was frequented by people who visited a favorite snorkeling spot nearby. Donuts and Tweety Bird took a vacant blue painted table. At another, two children were going through a stack of old magazines. Their father was helping them to identify the things that they pointed to. The wife, a hawk nosed Indian with unflinching eyes, stood behind the counter and said "Pepsi" when Donuts ordered "Dos Coca cola."

"Okay Pepsi."

"I don't want to drink in this godforsaken outpost," Donuts grouched.

"*Si*, I mean yes," Tweety said.

Donuts gave him a serious look, "Tweety, don't lose your English."

"It ain't likely," Tweety snickered as the two Pepsi's arrived with straws in each.

In his notebook Donuts jotted down the items that were for sale at the counter: blackened bananas, green oranges, powdered milk, chilles, a weird variety of candies and one jar of mayonnaise. Donuts had the woman empty the alien monster head decanter of candies into a bag and paid the price she asked. How could this couple be agents?

PORTS OF HELL

Donuts wondered. The Chief had said they weren't certain, but they had obtained a tip from a rogue. The woman at the counter looked at Donuts suspiciously. He caught the look and a hunch told him that indeed she was an agent. He wanted badly to please the Committee.

"Tweety," he said, "let's move on and wait for a taxi up there on the road." When they got a ways away an excited Donuts said, "They are agents, Goddamn it. We'll send a fax off today."

Tweety Bird wondered if he was right.

Malloy stirred with a menacing undercurrent in the thick brush. He watched Jamie almost dance down the incline to the small beach, dive in and swim out to an awaiting motorboat where he was hoisted aboard by two Mexicans. The boat disappeared behind some rocks. A botanist searching for some elusive plant suddenly appeared in front of Malloy and was going to say buenos diaz until he made eye contact and decided to say nothing. Malloy watched him walk away and a slow smile appeared on his fearsome face.

Mesmerized by the blinding sun Malloy drifted back to his drafting into the Committee, not so long ago, in the Philippines: Angeles City, to be exact, right after his bride-to-be had dumped him. He was walking the hot streets past the steaming, nameless messes stewing in pots. There were cat calls coming from loudspeakers amongst the red lights. Malloy paused by a crumbling archway; beyond was an area he was drawn to explore. In the little square he found an ornate chair fit for an emperor. He heard heavy boots behind him. Malloy watched a man near his own age, dressed in a black military uniform, sit down in the chair. The man spoke and his voice had a resonance Malloy had never heard before.

"You, my friend, have been elected to serve the Committee," he said. "As an IS." The man produced a pipe and a soft leather pouch of tobacco, tested the bowl and began to fill it. "The most exalted Enemy feels it's important for the elect to acknowledge agreement." He lit the pipe reflexively. "A vigorous transformation is in store you. Your longevity will be enhanced and life will never be the same again."

The man puffed his pipe and the fragrance of the fine tobacco drifted through the air reaching Malloy's nostrils. It represented to Malloy everything that was good in life and he yearned greedily for this new lease. At the same time Malloy was stunned by the extraordinary event. He did not know exactly what the man was

Part Two

talking about.

"The alternative," the man said calmly, "is to return you to your regular life and no memory of this meeting would survive."

Malloy did not believe this. "I'm your man," he said, trying to summon the old bravado he had mustered a few times in his life.

The man's creased face showed the vague hint of a smile. "Yes, I believe you are, Mister Malloy."

That was the last thing Malloy remembered with any coherence. The rest consisted of snatches of images that seemed too fantastic to be real. A disk was stuck into his mouth and disappeared down his throat. His tongue expanded six feet before him like some bug eating reptile. He was placed into an incubator and hurled off into a disturbing blackness; when Malloy finally emerged he was in a private hospital, just outside of Phoenix, Arizona. Malloy then underwent a series of scans, blood tests and x-rays before the man visited him again.

That time a doctor wearing a white smock and thick glasses had him get up and walk around the room. The man who would become known as the Chief was wearing a gray business suit and remained silent in a corner, making notes on an electronic note pad. The room went black and with a short pointer the Chief drew two luminous X's on his eyes. They blazed and spun there then disappeared into Malloy's head. Malloy remembered that soaring feeling of strength and youthfulness and the dark unnamable power that stirred within him. Malloy began the visual transformation to an IS. He became a hideous, wonderful creature and howled with an awesome black joy. Somehow he'd been transported to the underworld of the gods, where he always felt he'd truly belonged.

Malloy practiced the transformation daily. The Chief had given him the magic pointer; with one X he could leave his human shell behind and with leathery wings could fly above the city. The Chief told him that in this state he might be able to bring a "wondrous specimen" onto the planet. A week later he was whisked off to the airport in a limousine.

In one month, in Puerto Angel, he had brought two specimens in. Both had crawled out of his anus after he had transformed to an IS. This was a first, he was told: a complete specimen had never been brought in before.

There had been another near success and Malloy knew who had been responsible for thwarting it: Elias. And the writer guy from the plane was his new agent. Small, funny world he thought. He would destroy them both.

PORTS OF HELL

* * * * * *

At first, Tweety Bird thought Donuts was the owner of the yacht that had anchored in the bay during the night. He wore a pastel orange billed cap, blue-and-white striped trunks and a sedate white jersey with a collar. He wore tennis shoes and a fancy gold watch that Tweety had never seen before.

"Where's your wacky shirt, Donuts?"

Donuts harumphed, sat down, surveyed the beach, the table between them and finally Tweety. In sotto voce he said, "Should I remind you that we are undercover?"

"Huh, whatta'ya think I'm stupido?"

"Well, I suggest that you too change your appearance."

"I'm way ahead of you, Donuts. Way ahead of you."

"I see," Donuts said as he watched a dog rolling on its back in the sand.

An eight year old Mexican girl with the face of an ancient temple maiden approached with a covered plastic bucket. "*Empanadas, papaya, pina?*" she asked. Donuts and Tweety Bird simultaneously shook their heads no.

The pipe music of the Andes which Tweety always requested came over the restaurant's sound system. Donuts signaled Ecidro for a Corona. Tweety had failed to order one for Donuts and there was a grain of resentment in Donuts' attitude that remained the entire morning.

Two shapely, brown girls walked by in the surf. They wore black bra tops and printed sarongs tied sassily like exotic miniskirts. A group of deeply tanned backpackers walked by, wearing chic straw hats from Guatemala. A boy passed with a hefty, sleek tuna slung over one bare shoulder. The sun was all-powerful and the bay blue and sparkling like a dream painting come to life. The sound of the surf echoed across the bay. Above, the seagulls floated in the sky casting moving shadows on the beach. But something was off, Jamie felt. Something was out of place. He sipped his orange juice. Jamie thought about Tweety Bird and Donuts as he watched them. Then the realization came over him. Decoys. Paranoia crept over him because the IS had probably spotted him. He would now have to move to another cabin and swear the old proprietor to secrecy.

Doctor Hunter and his assistant sat at a open-air restaurant that was on a hill high above the beach. They were fit and tan and enjoying their fresh grilled tuna.

Part Two

* * * * * *

Later in the day, Tweety Bird reappeared on the beach and Donuts appraised his new look. He wore a pair of cutoff black pants and huaraches he had purchased in Pochutla and a white T-shirt with a green iguana that covered the front and advertised Puerto Angel. He wore a new pair of sunglasses that had a string to keep him from losing them. He was hatless and continued to wear the three gaudy silver rings. Donuts wasn't sure if he really looked any different but nodded his approval.

Nearby, two boys crouched by a wall and demonstrated rain sticks for an old German professor who had been suffering from diarrhea for two days and was on his way to the farmacia. He had stopped, suddenly fascinated with the sticks. He did not purchase one however, and frowned when he passed the duo and the row of empty Corona bottles.

"Fuck you too," Tweety muttered. "Some people are just never happy," said Tweety Bird the philosopher.

Donuts smiled and took a long pull on his beer. Tweety did the same and slammed it on the blue-and-white checkered table cloth that covered the table, causing the bottle neck to fill with foam. Donuts plucked a Montana from the pack and sighed with deep contentment. "You're absolutely right, Tweety. It certainly is a beautiful spot."

* * * * * *

Crescents of golden sand, singing waterfalls, beachcombers' wind-swept dreams of twisted driftwood and, beyond the reefs, the rainbow colored fish.

Roscoe had seen a sign for the Air Force station and a Marine Corps air station. After a couple of wrong turns he found HED Inc: three long, gray slabs of buildings surrounded by a lot and an electrical fence topped with barbed wire. Almost lurid "No Trespassing" signs everywhere. He drove back to the nearby crossroads: a store, a café, a gas station. He parked. Down the road he could still see the checkpoint at the entrance of HED Inc. Roscoe watched as a tarp covered truck pulled into the store's small lot. It had an HED Inc. sticker on the windshield.

Roscoe had placed the loot in a safe deposit box. The disk was in his pocket. He got it out and looked at it again, twisting it open. Inside on one piece was a red mirror. He screwed it back together and put it back in his pocket. Both occupants got out of the truck and went into the store.

PORTS OF HELL

He climbed in the back with a bunch of crates of supplies. A few moments later he heard voices and movement in the cab. The engine started and the truck rolled toward the compound. It stopped at the checkpoint. Would they check the back? Roscoe fingered the little black automatic. They moved on.

Roscoe peeked out the back at the guard, who was taking a drink from a styrofoam cup. He looked again and the coast seemed clear. The truck moved slowly across a parking lot. Roscoe hung from the back step, dropped off and walked casually into a side entrance of a building.

He found an empty dressing room: lockers, basins, mirrors, a hair dryer, a scale. He opened some of the lockers and found a blue work jumpsuit and a white hard hat like both the truck men and the guard had worn. He put them on.

Roscoe followed a corridor inward to the building's core. At a set of round doors with pink tinted windows he peered in; men dressed like him were gathered in lines in a large room. They looked mesmerized, like religious converts. Roscoe stepped back, seeing a foreman or guard walking about inspecting the lines. The men began to glow and the room fell into a murky green light. Above each of them floated a white ball of light.

The glowing men turned into jet black statues and the balls of light disappeared. The statues broke open neatly and what stepped out stunned Roscoe even more: gorgeous women, blondes, brunettes and redheads, curvaceous and naked.

After admiring each other's bodies, they fell into another line behind the minder, who called out instructions, and off they sauntered like trained horses. Roscoe felt as though he had entered into a world he had always relegated to pulp novels, fantastic illustrations and B-movies.

Roscoe took the first exit he saw and headed across a lot, looking for a car with keys in the ignition. He passed two men dressed like him who nodded and kept walking. He spotted keys and got in. Roscoe started the car and drove slowly towards the checkpoint. The old white haired guard asked for his "mirror." Roscoe took out the disk, opened it and showed him the red mirror. The guard's eyes widened and his expression became wild. Then something completely congruent with what Roscoe had been experiencing happened: the guard's head exploded. Roscoe stepped on the gas as an alarm went off behind him.

Should he go to the CIA? Or

Part Two

was it CIA operated? This thing was way out of his league. He was baffled: Other worlds? Time travelers? Whatever he had just seen was certainly connected to the queen in some way.

He took a couple of sleeping pills and in the morning got a message from Izzy the hacker that the Shields brothers had arrived at the Waikiki Hana. Roscoe called and Sonny answered and they agreed to meet in two hours.

After the scene at HED Inc. Roscoe was afraid to open the disk again. He drank some cold beer and ate a mahi mahi sandwich. Afterwards he smoked a Camel and picked his teeth clean. There was a loud knock at the door.

He looked out the absurd peep that made the Shields brothers look like they were thirty feet away. He opened the door said hello and invited them in.

There was something different about Sonny, Roscoe thought. The same wide shoulders and bullet shaped head. The same receded short gray hair. What was off? The eyes. Jet lag?

Sonny and Stan stepped in and glanced around. They both seemed nervous and cautious and they had come an hour early. Roscoe was trying to figure out what was wrong. He decided that it was not the Shields at all, but some sort of replicants. Sonny said, "You alone?"

"Well, yes, why?"

"Give us the fucking disk."

Roscoe backed away and they measured the distance between them. One forced a lopsided smile.

"Look," he said holding out a shield. "We're government, Roscoe. Committee. This is out of your field, just hand it over and we'll forget you held out."

"What about the money?" Roscoe asked to stall.

They both looked blank for a moment.

"Oh yeah," the other one said, "give us the money too, but first give us the fucking red mirror."

"The what?"

"Hand it over Roscoe," the Sonny one said as they moved towards him. They stopped when they saw the automatic.

"There's something fishy here boys, back off," Roscoe said and they looked at each other.

"We're government, Roscoe," they both said at the same time.

"We'll see," Roscoe said and relieved them of their guns. "Into the bathroom please."

They reluctantly obliged and Roscoe shoved a quick-lock device on the door. "I'm making a phone call," he shouted.

The hallway was empty. No elevator available. He ducked into a janitor's closet. A little while later he heard them come out. Evidently there was still no elevator, so they headed for the stairs.

Back in the room Roscoe finished his beer. He called Stevenson who gave him a number where he could reach him later. He threw his bag together and checked out by phone. After returning the rental he took a cab and found another room. He had Indian food for lunch and kept burping it the rest of the day. He called Stevenson back.

"Where are you?" Stevenson asked in what Roscoe detected as a funny tone: just something there in his voice that wasn't there before. Roscoe named another neighborhood entirely. "Uhuh, well those guys are for real, Dan, Washington D. C., top security. And the word is they're in contact with, hold onto your hat... aliens."

"I'm listening."

"Well, so this is very important," he said sounding not at all reassuring.

Roscoe let a little dead time pass then asked, "Why and how did the Shields brothers become government agents? And what's the deal with HED Inc. over in Lanikai? Who did Sal Shields? Do you know?"

"Roscoe, I don't really care," Stevenson said. "My instructions are to convince you to give up the disk."

Roscoe saw the Shields replicants coming down the street, moving in his direction. He hung up and got away before they spotted him. Back at his room he contemplated the situation. The whole thing had him confused and nervous. The disk? With a certain degree of apprehension Roscoe unscrewed it and chanced a look. He felt an immediate glow and quickly looked away. But he was drawn back and a red globe appeared in his mind's eye. Then it was as though he had been dropped into a pool of water. He found himself standing at the marina. A hefty man stood before him wearing a gray suit and a matching derby. The man had the most compelling blue eyes Roscoe had ever seen. His tiny teeth sparkled when he smiled. He held a golf club upside down as a cane.

"Elias is the name."

A jolt of recognition surged through Roscoe.

"Dan the man, welcome to what Mr. Lee used to call MU, the Magical Universe."

The next thing Roscoe knew they were in an ancient vessel at sea. Elias was saying something in his ear.

"We've bridged from Lemuria to today and the stars," Elias said softly. "The color here is yellow and it's referred to us the gathering place. HED Inc. is here to assimilate Committee replicants into the population."

Roscoe told Elias he would do whatever was required of him. He felt extraordinary. He had stepped into another world. He looked at a bright purple, pink lei floating in a puddle. The sun was reflected in the water.

"Deliver the disk to one of our agents in Mexico. It's imperative that he receives it. I'll take over here."

Elias pointed out to sea at an old freighter that had appeared on the horizon. An Asian boy wearing purple flowered trunks stood before them, smiling with crooked white teeth. Toon gestured to the small boat tied up nearby

ELEVEN

Lizards and more lizards scurried off in every direction when Malloy stepped onto the dirt and stone road. He cut up a burro path and even the lingering butterflies glided away. He crouched to the side of the compost closet that was ten feet or so from Jamie's first cabin.

When night fell Malloy sensed someone coming up the main path; he could see that it was not the agent, but the one who had appeared in front of him in the field. It was the botanist, still searching for his elusive plant; on a tip from Elario, he was coming to see the old proprietor. The botanist, however, had taken a wrong turn.

Malloy gazed stupidly at the moon. He looked lovingly at his hands, which were razor sharp claws, and crept towards the botanist. As the man started to knock at the door Jamie, doused in citronella oil and other scents the shaman woman had given him, popped up above a bush with a flaming bolt drawn back on the ComBow. He fired and the bolt stuck into the back of Malloy's bulky, macabre head. Malloy snarled and pulled it out, turning and searching for Jamie.

The botanist ran off down the mountain path. Feeling cocky, Jamie torched another bolt and fired but Malloy swatted it away as though it was an annoying bumblebee. He came for Jamie, who had just enough time to go back down the hole. Jamie waited a while before coming up again at another spot; Malloy was still whirling around, confused. He could not detect him as Jamie watched and quieted his breath.

Malloy choose not to go to the full IS change since his base form would be vulnerable to a savvy agent. He wondered if Jamie was that good or if he had backup. He decided to pass, to rethink and confer with the beloved Enemy.

"I know you now, Jim Jim," he yelled. "Sleep tight you little asshole, I'll find you in your goddamn dreams." Malloy stomped off, down the path returning to a completely human state, and like everybody else, he had to pull off cobwebs and get out his flashlight under the waning moon.

* * * * * *

The General, half bored, was staring at some graph on his computer screen. He took a drag off a joint that lay in a glass skull ashtray. He took a sniff of his 100-year-old brandy, swishing it gently in the snifter. He pulled a question mark across the screen and watched a map appear. A tangle of roads leading in all directions. He punched a call in.

"Hello?"

"Doctor?"

"General, what do I owe this pleasure?"

"Did you see the fax from Mexico?"

"Yeah, er, yes."

"What's the IS timetable?"

"He's got more than sixty hours left."

"Right. He's failed so far."

"Well not exactly. He brought in two specimens and he's still alive, although operations have shut down temporarily. But, really, Elias is not far away. We hope to do a double bill."

"Damn it. I want this operation on schedule. This is not the importation of sea cucumbers, for chrissakes."

"The IS will come through," the doctor pleaded. "He's taken on the local Capitan of the base and has men at his disposal."

"Very well doctor, ring me with any progress."

"Yes sir."

* * * * * *

Donuts' massive weight seemed to guide him as he made his way down the street to the Telemex where "Larga Distancia" and "De Fax" were advertised. He was displeased to see he had received no response to a fax sent two days prior. He questioned the owner, a man who had started the business three years ago with an even disposition but had since developed a harder edge to his demeanor. Donuts questioned his equipment and the man held his ground. "No reply *sénor*. You wish to send another or call?"

Donuts watched a white lizard on a wall doing pushups. The lizard turned upside down, went down the wall and disappeared. "No, no *gracias amigo*." After all, Donuts thought as he left, he didn't want the guy pissed off; an

Part Two

important message may come in or have to be sent. No reply meant something, he reasoned: to carry on, to continue to document reports—although neither of them had been back out to the cafe. Donuts realized they needed to return and try and find out more.

REBELS BLAST AND ROB COMMITTEE VAN

Phoenix, Arizona. An armored Committee van was destroyed with a rocket launcher and machine-guns early yesterday and one of its crew was killed. A large sum of cash and top security files were taken, police said.

Two other Committee personnel were wounded in the attack about nine miles outside of Phoenix. Neither the exact amount, nor what the files contained was disclosed. Police said more than ten armed and masked men took part in the attack, which appeared to have been carefully planned. About sixty spent shells were found on the ground afterwards.

The armored van had left the Phoenix Committee headquarters after collecting deposits and files when its way was blocked by two cars. When the guards refused to leave the van, the rebels opened fire and blew up the van's security door with a liquid explosive. A forty-five-year-old guard, father of six children, died in the blast, police said. The perpetrators sprayed a cryptic sign on the van of two circles connecting. This has been deciphered by one expert as a hobo sign for "don't give up."

Trisha Ladd of Against The Committee (ATC), was questioned by police in Washington D. C. In a press conference, she said the rebel attack was in no way connected to her organization and that the ATC was a peaceful movement that would pursue the Committee in the legal arena.

When asked about the recent demonstration that had turned violent, Ms Ladd answered, "The violence was provoked and engineered by the Committee itself and we will be proving that in the courtroom."

ATC was organized after Ms. Ladd's book, *The Enemy, The Committee and The Conspiracy*, was published last year.

* * * * * *

The Commander had eyestalks that wavered over his waxy, purplish rodentlike face. The eyestalks retreated into his head and thin, pale eyes looked out

PORTS OF HELL

over the massive, circular conference room where the tables slowly revolved. A yellow light dimly emanated from each table. The Commander sat on a tall stool and licked his leathery lips before he spoke. When he did, his bass voice resonated throughout the vast room.

"Can a specimen infused with X maintain life while drifting through the deadly environment of interstellar space? Our specimens are astonishingly hardy and seem able to repair damage to themselves that would instantly destroy all predecessors. They have survived 15,000 (1.5 million rad) of ionizing radiation. In mere hours, the models were reassembling their own chromosomes. They have bridged successfully, even after their armored capsules have been destroyed. Our IS has been able to receive two. One was extinguished. And the IS life span is quickly running out. Short time remains for it to give birth. And he has been sighted. We have a temporary delay.

"Three more have been released but they will unfortunately burn up in Earth's radiation and gravitational fields; however we feel that one of the organisms might have a chance of surviving in a random mutated, and hence unknown capacity. Of the original two, one with disk remains in holding."

The Commander stood, bowed slightly and stepped backwards until he disappeared through a door cut to the exact form of his body.

REBELS ON ATTACK

Washington, D. C. Led by the fiery Trisha Ladd, founder of Against the Committee (ATC), hundreds of demonstrators have caused substantial havoc at the Ronald Reagan National Airport after the assassination of Committee Chief Marshal Gittines. Three times that number of ATC activists convened at Committee Headquarters threatening to burn down the building and take more hostages. Pirate radio broadcasts urged looting and arson as "everyday citizens" vowed to become guerrilla fighters for ATC.

"They're trying to erase our dreams," an emotionally charged Ms. Ladd said in her live internet hookup. "We're seeing a polarization among the people: those who dream and those who do not care," said the charismatic British author. "We have been forced to become warriors against the Enemy and their puppets the Committee."

Government forces report they

Part Two

have squashed the uprisings although there is a news blackout on casualties and injuries. Trisha Ladd and her inner circle of Rebel ATC are being sought through all possible sources, a police spokesman reported.

* * * * * *

Tangolunda Bay, Huatulco. "The sea ez ruff tonight," was the report from Ariel, the quiet hotel boy with the faint smile.

Elias, or perhaps it was King Neptune himself, strode through the turbulent surf then swam the bay like some creature of the sea. Not unlike a dolphin, he leapt into the air then dove to a remarkable depth resurfacing back near the shore. An old vendor who was counting her bag of nuts, nanches and pumpkin seed packets crossed herself and asked for Jesus and Our Lady of Guadalupe's protection and blessings.

* * * * * *

Capitan Gomez boarded the motorboat and gloomily surveyed the bay. It was still a little rough and muddy from the previous night's storm. The sky was still overcast. The motorboat headed towards the yacht that had docked two days previous. He hated these inspections, such a bore, to search for what? Drugs? Pornography? Fugitives? There was never anything. The papers were always in order, but still it was part of his job. The owner would be waiting half drunk, with some bimbo, a big smile and the customary box of chocolates that, like everything else, had fallen into mundane formality.

They pulled aside the yacht; a man grabbed a rail but the new guy who manned the engine accidentally pulled the boat back and they all watched helplessly as the first man stretched between the two boats and fell, machine-gun and all, into the water. The rest of the men couldn't help but laugh, but quickly helped him back aboard.

Capitan Gomez looked at the new man who apologized and fumbled with the engine for a minute before regaining his composure. Again they approached the yacht, this time correctly. The dripping, hatless man growled a threat to the new man who blinked and remained silent. As the inspection took place, the Capitan found his thoughts elsewhere. Why hadn't Malloy contacted him? He, after all, was his ally. He had been primed and then nada. He was supposed to help Malloy, wasn't he? He decided to pay Malloy a visit that evening. Perhaps, he rationalized, that was what Malloy preferred.

PORTS OF HELL

* * * * * *

Hector and Jamie met on the beach and made their way back the trippy paths of Zipolite. They passed a rusted skeleton of an old Rambler. A clinging brown weed had attached itself and covered it entirely making it appear like a displaced piece of Surrealist art.

They climbed a path past some people camping. At the top were a group of colorful cabanas. Sleepy, healthy looking cats were sitting around on chairs. Jamie scratched their heads. Hector disappeared into a cabana and returned with a bag of huge marijuana buds. He dumped them on the table and began to manicure some. Hector said the weed was purchased from an old compesano who set up shop under a tree. This was an especially good crop.

Hector rolled a spliff apiece and they smoked, looking out over a grove of coconut palms that led to the ocean. Jamie took a nap in one of the hammocks.

Later, they went down to a beach restaurant to meet Anna. They dined on savory crepes and Dos Equis oscuras. Hector tossed down his first beer in a couple of gulps. He lit a fresh Cuban cigar purchased in Mexico City. He gestured around him with the match that had gone out.

"It's your usual expat community of drifters, dropouts, druggies and sickies."

Anna laughed.

Anna and Jamie took the local yellow school bus to Mazunte. They walked to the far end of the beach and climbed some rocks. There was a natural Jacuzzi formed within the rocks below, filled with benign, electric blue fish. It was a spectacular night; the sun setting and the moon coming up simultaneously.

"I'm off to Scotland," Anna said in his ear, "to help Trisha get settled."

Jamie kissed her gently across her eyebrows, causing her to shiver with delight.

He would see her off in Pochutla the following day.

* * * * * *

In the village of Puerto Angel, Jamie and Anna sat in a little cafe surrounded by red-and-white bougainvillea. They ordered lemonades. They found a mixture of turmoil, love and lust in each other's eyes. Jamie reached under the table and stroked her bare leg that was propped on his lap. He grasped the calf muscle and rubbed her ankle and tickled the soft skin under her knee.

"Let's get a cab right now," she said, excited.

A number of them were passing outside. Jamie tossed down

Part Two

some pesos and followed her into the street where she had already stopped one. After loading in her backpack, they sped off and Anna started to egg the driver on; "*Rapido. Muy rapido,*" she cheered. Already driving too fast, the driver floored it. They raced around the windy, zigzag roads to Pochutla. Anna became giddy. Jamie grabbed her breasts and squeezed them.

Traffic was backed up to the edge of town. They got out and climbed the narrow sidewalks. It was Monday, market day, and the streets were jammed. At the pink Izala Hotel, where the cabs waited for fares, they stood and looked over the tarp covered stalls at the market that spread out in each direction.

Taking Jamie's arm, Anna urged, "Let's get a room here, now." They went into the Izala's surprisingly clean lobby and arranged for one. Inside, Anna let her shorts fall to her ankles and kicked them away. She sat on a chair by the window, the bustling market below. She crossed a leg and made a weird expression. Then she began fingering herself and murmuring. "You can start here." she said. "I'll show you where I want your tongue." Jamie was already aroused.

After a while she started pulling his hair and talking crazily while Jamie used his fingers.

"Oh darling," Anna said when he began in earnest, "We're alive, and f-f-fucking at the Izala Hotel."

At the side of the dusty road Jamie watched the bus disappear. He was filled with an immense tenderness.

* * * * * *

Jamie was quite indiscernible from the other local young men in Puerto Angel. Deeply tanned, he also affected their style of baggy T-shirt, longer hair and a certain gait that had to be found naturally. He walked barefoot with toughened soles on any road or path. He had learned enough Spanish to get by as well as a smattering of Zapoteca. Early in the morning he practiced the squat under a tree full of Orioles.

In the cabin Jamie took off his straw hat and hung it on a peg. He had arranged a circle of candles around the bed and an outer circle of cacti. His longish hair fell into his eyes and he tied it back with a strip of leather. With a knife made from a goat's horn Jamie sliced his arm and smeared the blood across his chest. He laid down on the cot and folded his hands behind his head.

* * * * * *

Tweety Bird received a letter

from his sister with the extraordinary news that a distant uncle in Toronto had passed away and had named Thorton his sole inheritor. It converted to a substantial $58,734.

Donuts suggested that living in Mexico and buying the right stocks, they could live well for the rest of their lives. Tweety respected Donuts' know-how with business and agreed to make him his business partner. Donuts wanted him to open a bank account in Pochutla and then build a house. Elario the barkeep recommended they speak with a gringo who had done just that. Elario drew a map on how to get to Malloy's house.

Tweety Bird and Donuts decided to retire in Puerto Angel. They talked to the locals about land, building a house and the purchase of a VW bug. They had already bought a two-year-old Doberman named Hitler.

They would complete the assignment, then appeal to the General. They hoped to remain in this raw bit of paradise perpetually stewed in the beer and rum that were beginning to make Donuts' feet swell.

Donuts did a quick dancelike step to avoid the incoming tide from rushing over his tennis shoes. Tweety, who had wildly switched to margaritas earlier and had not eaten, lagged drunkenly behind. "McDonough, damn it! I've got a hell of a headache. Can't we do this some other night?"

* * * * * *

The General and the doctor sat in a sedate room except for the illuminated skull that decorated one wall. The General was agitated and drummed his fingers on the table. "So then, things are fucked."

The doctor felt the General's eyes would bore holes in his head if he didn't put him at ease. "Not so. Not so." The doctor took time to clean his glasses with a handkerchief and formulate what he was going to say to this fanatical half-alien.

"Not so my ass. First we have this English cunt causing nothing but problems. She's a goddamn pest. Second, our IS was bushwhacked and may not pull off the birth before he's history. I understand one of the other three specimens may actually make it, but be a walking whack job, and we'll have to do the stop ourselves."

The doctor put his glasses back on and tried to display the deep wisdom of a man who had absorbed the best from every school of psychology and philosophy and had refined it into one indisputable world view.

Part Two

"It's only a matter of time before Trisha Ladd is locked away for good and her joke revolutionaries forgotten," the doctor finally said. "And remember Malloy's high scoring? He's in motion as we speak."

The General tapped his hash pipe against his heel then picked obsessively at the bowl and blew through it a few times before he put it back in his vest pocket.

The doctor raised an index finger. "I predict that Operation Import will be successful once we get through this necessary rough patch."

The General pursed his thin bluish lips. "I certainly hope so, for both our sakes. Tomorrow I talk to the president and the next day a goddamn Commander. In fact..." there appeared a slight glimmer in the General's eye, "you, Herr Doctor, will accompany me." The General said this last statement with a satisfied smile.

The doctor pulled out a vial of cocaine and did a two and two. He looked at the illuminated skull on the wall and for a moment saw two of them floating there in front of him in the diffused light.

* * * * * *

Jamie's ComBow and knife were missing. He went through the arched entranceway of the cemetery of Puerto Angel. The sound of the bell registered a strong sense of déjà vu. His head was pulsing red. He began to climb the hills, glancing at the blue and green pastel, almost cartoonlike, crypts and tombstones there above the ground. The cemetery was suddenly alive with people wearing skull masks and carrying skull dolls and macabre puppets on sticks. They wore flashy clothes and danced about joyously drunk. A woman wearing a headband of dead lizards danced by. Was it Day of the Dead? He took a skull mask that was offered. And where was Malloy? Jamie made his way further up the hilly mounds. People offered him tamales, mescal and cigarettes. He sat behind a white tombstone that had an angel perched at its top. People were singing louder and louder while others whistled and yipped. Jamie placed the mescal and cigarettes on the ground and pulled up the mask.

Sick to his stomach, he crouched and vomited violently and then a second time. Malloy was coming down a path in his direction. Jamie vomited again. Malloy sported a line of lit candles on his shoulders. He had broken through the dream circle. Malloy had cacti sticking out of his ears and he too wore a skull mask atop his head. Jamie wanted to lay down but knew that he couldn't. He pulled the mask down and leapt into the dancing crowd.

Malloy, now with the wings of a prehistoric flying creature, hovered above the graveyard, recognizable only to Jamie. Jamie drifted down to the beach amongst the empty tables of the palapa restaurants. There was no one else around. Someone had left a fire over by some rocks; nowhere for it to spread. The necessary fire for the ritual.

A strange gun was laying there in the sand in a red plastic holster. As Jamie went for the gun he saw Malloy land further down the beach and frantically wave his wings back into arms.

Palm trees swayed slightly around the mythic scenario of monster and agent. The sky changed shades but the sea remained still and black. Jamie saw the fever sores that covered Malloy's face. Sweat dripped from his forehead.

The pistol in Jamie's hand jumped about as if it had a mind of its own; he looked at it uncertainly. He found his cheeks flushed with blood, the red glow washing through him. Even the hairs on his arms were red and glowing faintly and his heart pounded away in his chest.

Gloating, Malloy approached, his crooked face shining with viciousness in the weak light. Another face appeared out of some shadows: the face of Dan Roscoe. He tossed the disk into the air and it made a singing sound like a tuning fork. Jamie caught it and inserted it into the chamber of the gun. Malloy did a mad jig, unaware of the passing. "Now punk I'm gonna cut you wide open," he said to Jamie.

Jamie flashed back to a young gunslinger who had traveled and lived in this part of Mexico in 1866. The kid's name was Slinger Jim and he claimed to be from Lemuria. And Jamie became Slinger Jim and the odd holster was around his waist and the gun was in it.

As Malloy raised a spear gun a wild figure drew and fanned the pistol. The IS fell to the ground full of holes. Jamie stepped over and reached into Malloy's mouth and pulled out the other disk.

* * * * * *

Capitan Gomez took a swig from his spiked canteen and watched in horror as Malloy's human shell turned into a mass of jelly that shrunk with small screams until it was gone. Dr. Hunter, dismayed as well, looked as though he might weep. Gomez drew his gun when he heard Donuts' knock at the front door. Tweety

Part Two

Bird still lagged behind and wondered if he was imagining the glowing vines that covered the ground and the two dead dogs. A drunken and deranged local family, armed with machetes, were making their way through the woods. They had decided to finally deal with this devil, this cascarrabias who lived in the house that shook. The Capitan headed out the back way and took a path that would lead him to the road. Calver and Hector sat there in a jeep and listened to the Expeller and watched for him.

* * * * * * *

Summer had arrived. The heat was thick, not a breeze in the entire state of Oaxaca. The colors of the bougainvillea, red, yellow, pink, purple and white, unmoving in the thick air like some heady Impressionist vision. Dan Roscoe studied an old map spread out on the wooden table. Jamie felt his shaved head and thought about Anna earlier walking along the beach. A young boy had held an umbrella for her. She had been topless and wearing a loose turban and a long sarong like some wandering Babylonian princess.

"Mexico has changed a lot since this map was made," Dan said and stretched and yawned. "Yes, but there are places on this map that are on no other," Jamie was quick to add. Elias and Winks were at the market buying garlic and the catch of the day. They would all dine under the new stars.

ABOUT THE AUTHOR

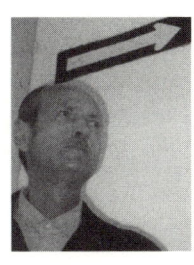

Johnny Strike has been published in a number of journals including *Headpress* and *Ambit*. He is a founding member of the influential US punk band Crime. He is currently at work on a second book set in Morocco. (Photo: Gregory Ego)